TRAP

AND OTHER FATEFUL TALES

By

JOHN MARGERYSON LORD

TRAFFORD
USA • Canada • UK • Ireland

All the characters and situations in these stories are purely imaginary, and any resemblance to any person living or dead is unintended.

© Copyright 2006 by John Margeryson Lord
All rights reserved. No part of this publication may be reproduced, stored in a retrieval system, or transmitted, in any form or by any means, electronic, mechanical, photocopying, recording, or otherwise, without the written prior permission of the author.

Note for Librarians: A cataloguing record for this book is available from Library and Archives Canada at www.collectionscanada.ca/amicus/index-e.html
ISBN 1-4120-8652-3

Printed in Victoria, BC, Canada. Printed on paper with minimum 30% recycled fibre. Trafford's print shop runs on "green energy" from solar, wind and other environmentally-friendly power sources.

TRAFFORD
PUBLISHING

Offices in Canada, USA, Ireland and UK

Book sales for North America and international:
Trafford Publishing, 6E–2333 Government St.,
Victoria, BC V8T 4P4 CANADA
phone 250 383 6864 (toll-free 1 888 232 4444)
fax 250 383 6804; email to orders@trafford.com
Book sales in Europe:
Trafford Publishing (UK) Limited, 9 Park End Street, 2nd Floor
Oxford, UK OX1 1HH UNITED KINGDOM
phone 44 (0)1865 722 113 (local rate 0845 230 9601)
facsimile 44 (0)1865 722 868; info.uk@trafford.com
Order online at:
trafford.com/06-0408

10 9 8 7 6 5 4 3

Dedication

This book is dedicated to Anthony Trollope. Tony was my friend and workmate for many years during which we spent most lunch breaks at one of several local hostelries. It was during one of these periods of sanity the basis for 'His Greatest Moment' evolved and created the idea for this family of short stories. Tony was a lovely man and I still miss his sound common sense and his dry humour.

CONTENTS

HIS BIG MOMENT 1
SECRET LONGINGS 13
THE BEAST 20
HOW HE GOT HIS BIRD 25
HE SOLD EVERYTHING 31
CHIMERA 39
THE FARM 47
THE VISIT 55
BACK FROM THE BRINK 62
PAST REGRETS 70
POWER 78
THE SUPER RUNNER 88
A HOLIDAY TREAT 95
A QUIET WOMAN 101
TOO GOOD TO BE TRUE 108
GOD'S MYSTERIOUS PLAN 114
FOR WANT OF WEALTH 122
THE LECTURE PRIZE 131
THE TRAP 138
THE WAY MONEY GOES ROUND 148

❦ **HIS BIG MOMENT** ❧

*G*erald Handle was not given to wild extravagant imaginings of glory and gratification. In forty years of struggle to maintain an acceptable standard of survival any such dreams had leaked out of him.

Until, that is, he won the Lottery!

Even then his smooth continuance was interrupted by only one unusual and dramatic incident.

Born one hundred per cent masculine, as far as he knew, he had started out in life with all the normal desires.

After a very few early exploratory and unsuccessful fumblings with the opposite sex, he had drifted into marriage with a friend of a friend, and; some years later and without a single memorable event had drifted out again; only to find himself living on his own without having sampled any of life's richer experiences.

He worked for a small insurance company in the suburb of one of our northern industrial cities.

A dull and conventional office job brought him regularly into the company of lady office staff. The men he hardly noticed nor they him.

Regaining batchelordom encouraged him to try his hand with the girls, after all he had seen others do it, it happened all the time on television and always looked remarkably easy.

He certainly tried very hard.

Firstly, and most obviously, was Jane. Jane was comely, warm, friendly, and even to Gerald's dormant emotions, undisguisedly sexy. Gerald had witnessed other members of staff chat her up - even the much pimpled junior clerk - but with what ultimate success he did not know. Still it seemed a natural place to begin. Such was her easy disposition that his initial moves looked as if they were going to bring a reward that made him tremble at the thought. He took her to lunch, sqeezed her hand under the table, swapped some very intimate personal details, and he even received several heart stopping kisses.

Thus encouraged, at one of their lunch-time meetings he tentatively suggested dinner at his place. Her totally unexpected reaction stunned him and set him back weeks.

'Not bloody likely!' She exclaimed. 'You might not be married, but I certainly am. My old man is very jealous, and if he got the slightest hint I was carrying-on he would kill me……. and probably you as well. 'Sides I'm not sure I fancy you all that much love.'

This last said as if she had only just considered the possibility.

The lunch-time jaunts were at an end, and working days were somewhat painful to Gerald after this, he felt that behind every door people were talking about him. He was very sensitive to nudgings and gigglings and felt great shame and embarrassment.

Gerald's next attempt at seduction, this time the tall, slim, well dressed Celia, happened almost by accident.

He noticed her getting on his bus each morning, and of course she took the same short walk from the bus stop.

Smiles and 'Good morning.'s were exchanged, and continued at this formal level for several months, until one day, on a very full bus, she sat next to him. Polite conversation led to discussions of shared interests. Likes and dislikes were very much in accord. But what to do next?

Then fate again took a hand, this time in the incongruous shape of his boss. Gerald was assigned a task which brought him into daily contact with the very source of his latest amorous phantasies. This in turn led to shared lunch-time sandwiches and combined attacks on the daily crossword, and this eventually gave him courage to try to bring his yearnings to reality.

Sadly his hopes were once more doomed to frustration. He was entertained to a very long and serious lecture in which his natural feelings were laid bare as base animal cravings which had no part in the friendship she entertained for him.

Work ground on.

Small hopes were raised by Jan and Joan. Young, inseparable, always clinging intimately to each other, they took an interest in him. However his half-hearted attempts to pursue one were always thwarted by the other, and he didn't dare offer himself to both at once.

Sally was always worrying about her several children.

Helen and Pam would never take him seriously.

Judith just ran and henceforth refused to speak to him.

Gerald even found himself taking an interest in Olive who's ancestors came from Africa, and who simply laughed at his feeble white man's attempt at seduction.

Failure now seemed certain, and was made more insufferable by his having to watch daily interactions between these ladies and the other male members of staff, which, superficially at least, seemed to be much more successful than his own.

Time wore on.

Then quite suddenly and unexpectedly - he won the National Lottery!

In spite of the fact that nothing as exciting as this had ever happened to him, Gerald looked at the cheque with its row of six noughts after the three almost without emotion. In fact its significance did not immediately dawn on him. He could not imagine life in any way different from his normal daily routine. - Get up, plod through the working day, go home, watch tele, go to bed. It was a very familiar and comforting existence.

Nevertheless it gradually sank in that at least he might take a holiday, even a long holiday, he might even find a more satisfying job; and so, with some fear and trepidation he decided to hand in his notice. He was as startled as were his colleagues to see himself take this step.

Thus emboldened, he decided to mark his leaving with something of an event. - But what? - A party? Although this idea was appealing, it was tinged by many unhappy memories of finding himself in corners enviously watching others making merry and flaunting their familiarity with the opposite sex.

And then he hit on it!

A party it would be - But, without the men.
A party with all the ladies to himself.
One in eye for the others.
The idea became more satisfying with contemplation.

To his amazement all the women accepted the invitation. Knowledge that he had won the Lottery, the promise of a special gift, and curiosity were sufficient inducements; and anyway, as Jan and Joan reassured each other, there was safety in numbers - wasn't there?

It was fully arranged at the local hotel for the evening of his leaving, and when it arrived Gerald found himself invaded by an excitement and a surging of blood he had not felt for many years.

Goodbyes to the men were said solemnly with many good wishes and lots of 'You lucky devil'.

Later at the hotel awaiting the first arrivals, the long table set out for the grand meal he had ordered, Gerald became very nervous. Would they all come? Would any of them come?

Very soon he was much happier. Singly and in pairs they started to arrive, and quite quickly the bar was merry with chatter and laughter. They all came, and Gerald was pleased and considerably flattered that each had changed from office clothes and the room was a joyful sparkle of jewelry and pretty dresses. Indeed they had done him proud for there seldom was a more colourful parade.

Drinks loosened tongues and the atmosphere became truly party-like. The meal got underway and was soon voted a success, and during coffee when all had drunk and eaten well he was called upon to make his speech. It was then he sprang his surprise.

'Ladies!' He began.

'Thank you all very much for coming, and if I may say so thank you all for looking so stunning.' - Applause.

'I can't say that I have always enjoyed working for the firm; but any pleasure I have had was because of you.'
- Cheers.

'You have been promised a little gift, and this is the time to reveal all.' - More cheers.

'Unfortunately there is only one prize, but you will all have an equal chance to claim it.' This was greeted with Oh's and exclamations.

'My little offering consists of a share of my Lottery win.' - Loud cheers.

'And,' he paused..........'Me.'

The room exploded.

'We don't want you - just the money.'

'I knew there was a catch in it.'

'Swiz.'

But no one left

'The idea is,' he continued, 'I am going to hold a reverse auction. I intend to start calling out amounts of money which will be your present for spending a few hours of love with me.'

Complete silence greeted this statement. 'And the first person to say yes will be the proud owner of the money...... and me.'

This, he thought, is where they all walk out. But despite the incensed discussion which broke over him like a wave; no one moved.

'Who does he think he is?'

'And us married ladies!'

'Bloody Casanova.'

'He must be mad, or joking.'

The good humour of the evening was somewhat restored by the arrival of the champagne, and the girls sure that none of them would fall for his proposition settled down for a good laugh.

Gerald took a good drink, a deep breath, and started.

'Fifty pounds.'

- Jeers.

'We're worth a lot more than that lad.'

'A hundred pounds.'

- More jeers.

'You will have to do better than that mate.'

'Two hundred pounds.'

- Jeers and laughter.

'You wouldn't get a sniff of my little toe for that.'

At five hundred pounds one or two were beginning to think that he might be serious after all.

'One thousand pounds.'

This was clearly a nice sum to be going home with for just a few hours of what might even prove to be fun; and one or two were beginning to consider the implications, and whether or not they should leave before the temptation became irresistible, but they let nothing of this show.

Some taunted each other.

'Go on Jane, you might even enjoy it!'

'Two thousand pounds.'

At this point he had their undivided attention, and to emphasise that his offer was genuine, he took out his cheque book, opened it, and laid it on the table with his pen.

'Ladies!' He said, 'I can hardly withdraw now with so many witnesses.'

He allowed this to sink in. Actually Gerald was both amazed and alarmed that his plan had got this far. Turning dreams into reality like this was both exciting and daunting. And he was now not sure that he could go through with it. He felt that he had already bitten off more than he could chew, but found that he could not now loose face by stopping what he had started.

The girls, on the other hand, were each considering their own situations. More than one of them, if they had been on their own, would have given in by now; but to do so publicly was preventing them. Several were weighing the risks, aware that sooner or later there must come an offer which, publicly or not, could not be refused. But who would be first and claim it?

Such was the party atmosphere that the girls did not even consider that they were being asked to put a value on their honour. They never dreamed of any likeness between themselves and professional ladies. Fundamentally the money and curiosity were holding them.

'Three thousand pounds.'

'Oh dear!'

This was from Sally. She was thinking that for her this was a very rare treat - new clothes for the kids and something left over for herself. She went quite pink and realising that all eyes were on her turned rapidly from pink to red. She made strenuous efforts to convince everyone that she had no intention of saying yes. She was not believed, so this was the first admission that anyone had seriously considered the proposition and might even be prepared to go through with it. This shocked them all, including Gerald, and sealed the contest.

The competition was now definitely on.

'Three thousand five hundred.'

Agitated whisperings from the inseparable pair.

Wildly Gerald pictured himself with both girls at once, but in the midst of curious and amazed looks from the others, the pair blanched and became silent.

Food and drink were now forgotten, and the girls regarded each other keenly whilst endeavouring at the same time to disguise their own feelings.

'Four thousand pounds.'

'Jesus!'

This from Jane who felt that this was more than she would earn in many months, and she might enjoy the experience, but the thought of what her husband would do to her if he ever found out held her back.

'Four thousand five hundred.'

Celia, normally icily composed, began biting her nails.

This is it! Gerald thought. But though he waited - she was silent.

At this point an urgent need caused Gerald to excuse himself and leave the fray, Whilst relieving himself he gleefully considered which girl would be his. For now it appeared to him to be an absolute certainty and only a matter of time. He discovered that his nervousness had gone, and he returned to the party feeling very much the conqueror.

But - on returning he became immediately aware of a change in the atmosphere. The girls were now sitting quietly chatting, and the tensions which had earlier pervaded the room seemed to have evaporated. His control of the situation had in some indefinable way been lost.

They now regarded him with polite cool smiles and waited patiently for him to continue.

Very unsure now, and feeling that they were about to make a joke of him, he tentatively began again.

'Er..........four thousand five hundred pounds.'

- Polite Silence.

'Five thousand.'

- Polite silence.

'Five thousand five hundred.'

- No response.

'Six thousand.'

- Still no response.

He hesitated.

- 'Do go on please,' someone said.

'Six thousand five hundred.'

- Polite silence.

At seven thousand his nerve broke, and he again hesitated. Clearly something was going on of which he had no knowledge, and the feeling grew that they had planned some terrible demise for him. There could not be any doubt that he was no longer master of the situation. His erstwhile confidence turned to cold fear, and he decided to stop.

Almost as one however the girls found their voice.

'Please go on.'

'Don't stop now.'

'You promised.'

The clamour partly soothed his anxiety, and timidly now he went on.

'Seven thousand five hundred.'

- Silence
This was ridiculous, he must stop now.

Gerald's growing discomfort was in contrast to the girl's clear enjoyment of the game. Realising that Gerald's waning courage was about to terminate the game, the girls ordered him a double brandy, and whilst he was fortifying himself with this they sought to encourage him to go on.

Under this pressure Gerald decided with some reluctance to press on, but made up his mind that he would definitely call a halt at ten thousand pounds. With this decision came considerable relief, it was not the money that was the problem, there was plenty of that, but the feeling that the girls were about to make a fool of him. He could now see an end to the game which had clearly mis-fired.

'Nine thousand five hundred.'

- Murmers of encouragement.

'Ten thousand.'

With this, and to his astonishment came a shrill -

'Yes please.'

***

Later, just before midnight in the large upstairs suite he had hired, he handed the last of the girls her cheque for her share, and called her a taxi to take her home.

They had teased him, seduced him, and finally made love to him until he could take no more. All his senses had been fully exploited and his whims gratified. For the first time in his life he felt complete. He realised that there would never be another day like this in the rest of his life and that his future had been changed for ever.

As for the girls - they had explained to him, what other way would ensure that they all kept the night's events secret, and of course share the prize, and if Gerald told anyone, who would believe him?

JML
2/6/2005

⇜ **SECRET LONGINGS** ⇝

*I*t was the evening of the first Thursday in December and Austin Morris's body quivered with an excitement that he was desperate to keep from his wife. To this end he did his best to keep out of her way busying himself with invented tasks around the house in places where she was not. This was hard work and he found himself ardently wishing she would hurry up and leave. But he dare not suggest this and tried to ignore the fact that she would take her time getting ready.

For some months now his wife had taken to having a night out with the girls on the first Thursday of every month, which if her mood the next day was anything to go by she thoroughly enjoyed, and it was now a fixture of their mutual routine.

A good education had given Austin the opportunity to land a very well paid job, and this was the reason that his very attractive young wife had targetted him for marriage, had lured him, and landed him. It might have been love on his part but his wife had soon made it clear that as far as she was concerned it was mostly a business arrangement. If it was affection he wanted it would have to be earned.

When on the rare occasion she decided to give him a little of her favours, usually after he had obtained a good pay rise or achieved some other business success, their love making was a very practical and unemotional affair leaving him feeling frustrated and alone.

In fact that aspect of life was frowned upon. She rarely laughed and often tut-tutted if he ventured to relate a slightly smutty joke he had picked up at his place of work.

By nature very highly sexed and normally inclined he had a certain roving eye and enjoyed many a voyeuristic gaze when he thought that his wife's attention was elsewhere engaged. But on the occasions that she caught him in the act her disapproving silence could last for several days.

He had some time ago come to the conclusion that his wife was an unemotional and even cold individual not much given to letting herself go in fun and loving.

But he knew that in all other aspects she was an excellent house keeper as his very clean neat and tidy house bore witness.

However life's pressures forced him to find a harmless outlet for his frustrations, and one which would be acceptable to his wife.

To this end he had bought himself a top of the range computer system with all the up date software, imaging, and photographic facilities. In this his wife had given him considerable encouragement, even assisting him in converting one of the spare bedrooms into a very acceptable study in which his computer had pride of place.

And let it be said in truth that his new found toy gave him an immense amount of pleasure after work when he would spend many absorbing hours lost in the interactive world of the computer - it became his salvation. It also had the advantage of keeping him out of his wife's way.

After some time of trial and error he became quite an expert with his machine. Net surfing became routine, and he was delighted and enthralled at being able to bring moving pictures onto his screen from all over the world and covering all manner of subjects.

It was during one such session that he had accidentally stumbled on a rather special website the content of which had taken him completely by surprise and which he had to hurriedly exit as he heard the key in the front door on his wife's return.

It had taken a few Thursdays since to remember how to access this site.

Clearly designed for lonely individuals like himself it was highly erotic in content providing as it did pictures that left very little and often nothing to the imagination.

So charged with guilt, these Thursday evenings became times of illicit pleasure much anticipated month by month. On his wife's return she would enquire as to what he had managed to learn from his evening's activities, and he often had considerable difficulty in providing her with a convincing story.

On this particular pre-Christmas Thursday his wife came downstairs and busied herself in leaving preparations, and Austin could not help observing that she was rather well and expensively dressed, and that she was still a very attractive woman, her early slim figure having now bloomed she was just the sort of female he letched after. He sighed to himself with deep regret that their life together had reached the stage of emotional stagnation, and wondered for the thousandth time where it had gone wrong.

As she was about to leave she regarded him sternly and admonished him to look after himself.

'As it's the last outing before Christmas the girls are planning something special so I will probably be a bit later than usual, so don't wait up.' Were her leaving words as she gave him a cursory peck on the cheek.

He knew that he would be asleep on her return as for him he had work in the morning and his day would start early with a cup of tea taken up to his wife in bed.

Minutes later he heard the door of her car slam and at last the sound of its engine fade away as she left him to his own devices.

He knew that he now had the whole evening to himself so he didn't rush upstairs to begin his much anticipated entertainment, he decided to relax and pour himself a drink and savour the thrilling sensation of holding himself back.

Whilst enjoying this tiple he contemplated what he would do when he finally switched on his machine and he decide that this time it had to be something special.

Trembling he mounted the stairs and on his way to his 'study' he passed his wife's bedroom (he had his own) and glancing in he noticed with a sudden feeling of sadness her matronly woollen nighty laid out on her bed, a stark contrast to the frilly, lacy item he had bought her in what seemed a long time ago. He noted yet again how well she maintained their house as he glanced at the spotless state of his own room, in this sense she was a model housewife for which he was ever grateful; he would in fact not know how to manage without her as the domestic scene did not appeal to him in the least.

At last. He was sitting in his chair opposite the screen with fingers poised over the keyboard ready to begin. Glancing at his watch the time was such that his wife would now be unlikely to return as she once had for some forgotten item and almost caught him with a screen full of erotic images of which she would have definitely had something to say.

It had at the time shaken him badly.

His fingers rattled on the keys and clicketty clicked on the mouse, and in just a few minutes the menu he sought was displayed.

Now the exercise he was about to indulge in was obviously quite expensive, there were various choices each of which had an associated price, thus the first thing he had to do to gain further access was to input the details of his credit card so that the machine could charge him for each item selected. So that this transaction would not turn up in their joint account and alert his wife, he had started his own secret account fed from time to time by odds and sods left over from the weekly allowance agreed with his wife. This had by now become a sizeable amount which he was about to exploit.

However!

This was the moment when he sowed the seeds of a future disaster!

He withdrew his wallet of cards from his pocket, and, in his excitement he withdrew the wrong card, and anxious now to get on, he quickly typed in the numbers from their joint account card, and returned the card to his wallet totally oblivious of his mistake.

The first menu on the screen was actually free, it showed a series of girls in full length pose, and asked him to choose and click on the girl of his choice. Although the girls were sexily dressed they wore face masks to disguise their identities. These were the girls of which one of them was about to perform for him for his pleasure.

Now all the girls were attractive and as he scanned them he was rather spoilt for choice, but eventually he picked the one who was just a bit more comely than the rest.

According to the screen she was called Celia.

So he clicked on Celia and was rewarded with a second menu listing a number of activities she would perform for him each with its corresponding price.

He was in for a long session and so decided to start with the least exotic item and work his way through the complete list.

This was a truly erotic striptease down to just two small items of clothing. As the striptease advanced he was increasingly entranced by the lovely figure this girl teasingly revealed. Voluptuous and full bosomed she displayed a body that he was greedy to see more of.

As she arrived at the minimum of clothing he was intrigued and amused by the fact that because of the season her last intimate coverings were enhanced by a fringe of purple and silver tinsel that danced and sparkled in the lights as she danced.

After this he moved steadily down the menu asking her to indulge in more and more increasingly erotic acts finishing up with a very naked and lovely lady writhing on a bed giving herself pleasure - and she was obviously enjoying it as much as he.

The whole experience lasted a couple of hours at the end of which she turned to the screen and wished him good night and without thinking he returned the greeting.

Switching off, he sat for some time gazing at the blank screen unable at first to drag himself away.

But he was soon in bed and relaxed to dream of - guess what?

***

Much later his wife quietly slid her key in the door, silently opened it and slipped inside, removed her coat and crept up to her room. As she mounted the stairs a single small strip of purple and silver tinsel fluttered down and lay glittering on the tread.

JML
12/6/2005

THE BEAST

It had been rumoured persistently and for some considerable time in the straggly village which sat on the very edge of a vast wild moor, that a large animal was roaming free in the wilderness. Some said there were more than one. In fact so strong was the rumour that most villagers took it as fact. The more remote routes across the moor were assiduously avoided and were rapidly becoming overgrown with natural vegetation.

Pub talk was of people being attacked by such a beast, but as these reports were always about strangers to the village hard evidence was not forthcoming. Old George from his special bar seat would, when oiled by the offer of a pint, relate his tale of an unknown man who came staggering off the moor bleeding and muttering incoherently and whom he helped to his parked car. As he drove away George thought he heard the man utter 'The beast!'

But the villagers knew old George and noted with considerable doubt that his experience took place after throwing out time.

The school master would quote (as he often did to any who would listen) his favourite poet.

'As D.C. Vault had it, 'Yon wild and witherly waste, is home to many wilderly baste.' he would loudly proclaim.

'Electrifying don't you think?'

And although the discussion would grow intense there was never anyone present who could claim having clearly seen a large wild animal on the loose although many knew of someone who had. Descriptions varied but most involved a large animal, brown, or black, or striped tiger like, lurking silently through the undergrowth.

Both local and national press had sent reporters to the village, and these too came back with nothing but tales of sightings and no pictures.

Thus the villagers avoided the moors as much as possible and only visiting walkers and persons from other places crossed the moor and kept the paths open.

However.

On one glorious autumn morning, Jane and Mary Ann set off along one of the more remote and wooded paths across the wilderness where they knew the best blackberries were to be found.

They did of course know well of the tales but in discussing it between themselves had concluded that rumours were all they were, thus although they ventured forth considerably warily they carried, in addition to their fruit baskets, a plastic bag containing their only defence should the stories be fact.

And so they set off along the winding path through the trees and patches of open scrubland. The day was pleasantly warm and with sunlight that played hide and seek with small patches of white cloud.

Squirrels ran and jumped across the grassy ground and dashed about the branches and trunks of nearby trees. The air was alive with bird song.

Strolling into one such sun-dappled glade they were surprised and somewhat startled to find a man leaning on a tree and observing them with some interest. He was clearly expecting them as the binocular strung round his neck attested to the fact that he had been observing them for some time. By his side and within easy reach was a double-barrelled shot-gun whose barrel gleamed metallicaly in the sunshine. He was dressed for the outdoors and was obviously comfortably at home in this environment, his attitude being one of relaxed amusement as if he was contemplating some unspoken joke. His face held a smile which although it was open was in some undefinable way not quite pleasant to observe.

'Well now lovely ladies, what might you be doing out here in this dangerous place?' he said, so softly that they only just caught the words.

The girls did not move or answer him.

They were village girls and knew everyone who lived there if not by name at least by sight - and this was no villager.

'Don't you know about the wild animal on the loose around here?' he asked equally quietly. 'You really shouldn't be out here all alone.'

The girls were taken so much by surprise that they remained silent.

Picking up the gun the man strolled slowly across the soft grass towards the now frightened and trembling girls whilst looking them up and down taking in every nuance of their youthful figures little disguised by their scanty warm weather outfits.

Both girls felt naked as he stood over them his smile now a stiff grin.

They stood like this, a little statue like group, for what to the girls seemed like an age. Then just as they thought he was about to leave them, his whole demeanour changed. His face grew red suffused with blood and his eyes took on a cruel, haunted, look; and he waved the gun and shouted.

'Get those bloody clothes off you whores.'

Startled the girls did not move and this increased his rage as if he would burst with pent- up fury.

'Did you hear me?' He spat the words out whilst waving the gun in their faces.

'Do it!'

The girls each reacted differently. Mary Ann much the younger started to cry whilst Jane grew angry and showed the man a defiant, scornful face. But they started to undress.

The man now manhandled each girl in turn with his intentions clearly on rape, his approach being hard vicious and uncompromising he was out to humiliate the girls as well as take his pleasure of them. All the time the gun was within his easy reach.

The girls were frightened for their lives and terribly abused. But whether it was due to Jane's scornful attitude to the man's attempts or to Mary Ann's persistent weeping he failed in his ambition to achieve his goal with either girl.

This made the man seethe and swear in frustration and grabbing the gun he waved it at the girls, who thought their end was upon them.

'Get to hell out of here you bloody miserable tarts before I blow your stupid brains to pieces,' he yelled.

By now both girls were equally distraught but managed to don the minimum of clothing and grabbing the rest scrambled sobbing and stumbling away from the scene as fast as they could, baskets and bag forgotten. They ran for their lives and as they did the man fired both barrels at their retreating forms. He missed but was so close that the girls heard the pellets as they hissed past only inches away.

The stranger gathered himself together and looking round spotted the unused baskets and beside them the plastic shopping bag bulging with its contents.

He leaned the now empty gun against a tree, lifted the bag and curious as to what it contained started to open it.

***

The very last thing he saw before he died were two large haunches of raw meat, and the last sound he heard was the crunch of four large canine teeth as they bit into his spine at the back of his neck.

Some distance away now the two girls heard his dreadful scream. They looked at each other and knew exactly what it meant. They slowed to a walk - no need to hurry now.

JML
26/6/2005

❧ HOW HE GOT HIS BIRD ☙

*J*im and Felicity Pringle were happily married, that is, until Jim retired.

They had successfully raised two children one of each sex both of whom had honoured them with healthy grand children which they occasionally saw when holidays and other commitments allowed.

Jim had a well-paid job in engineering having reached the dizzy heights of senior manager. He derived much satisfaction from his work which continually presented him with new and often seriously difficult challenges. He was often required to solve problems in the company's other centers around Britain and sometimes abroad; in this he had a wide range of close business acquaintances many of whom he entertained at home.

Felicity was not only a good parent but was also an excellent entertainer, a fact much appreciated by Jim, and whilst these occasions were very pleasurable, they were strictly business.

But Jim's schedule often left his wife with a certain amount of free time in which she had developed a significant circle of friends with whom she had much in common.

And so they lived in these separate worlds which only occasionally overlapped - that of Jim's work and his colleagues, and that of Felicity's domesticity and her friends.

Their love-life had by now reached that stage in life in which it could best be described as 'comfortable'. Whilst not exactly regular they both enjoyed what they had, although when Jim had tried occasionally in the early days to be more adventurous Felicity had gently but firmly guided him down their well practiced path to mutual satisfaction.

Although they were both attractive, neither Jim nor Felicity were tempted to stray; and their exclusive aquaintances, Jim's mostly male, Felicity's female did not present any such risk.

Life was good; stable; dependable and interesting if somewhat lacking in sheer excitement.

There was no hint as to the drama about to enfold, and inevitably no power on earth would divert it.

It started innocently enough as Jim's company announced a change of management at head office. But this was quickly followed by a merger with a much larger outfit involved in similar products. And out of the resulting reorganisation Jim suddenly and totally unexpectedly was made redundant together with most of the older members of his team.

It shook Jim to his very core. It was as if his whole reason for existence had been deleted. Sadly Felicity was of little help, merely assuring him that he would soon find other employment. But he didn't. His age and the salary he wanted were against him. Eventually he was able to negotiate a reasonable deal which gave him early retirement. But this at fifty five was not what he had in mind nor had given even a moments thought to.

And so one Monday he found himself at home with no hobbies or outside interests and nothing to do. His job had taken his whole attention.

At first Felicity was tolerant of his following her about the house asking if there were any jobs she wanted him to do, but he interrupted her routine and she soon made it plain that he was in the way.

He found that his acquaintances were just that and were only interested in business not friendship - it was as if he had the plague. Felicity on the other hand still had her girl's group and she now left the house more often just to get out of Jim's way.

The atmosphere in the house became tense and adversely affected their lovemaking - it became sadly infrequent.

After one day of frustration on both their parts Felicity made it plain that he had better take up some interest which would take him out of the house or she might leave.

Thus it was that fate gave the screw a further turn!

Jim had one good mate who's prime interest in life was bird watching, and Jim seized on this as a way out. So it was that he joined his friend's group and started to go on their outings and attend the lectures. Being the man he was he took a real interest, bought himself a good binocular, bought the identification books and became quite knowledgeable.

This relieved the pressure at home, and there things gradually returned to something like normal.

As Jim's outdoor experience grew he found he wanted something more than just watching, he wanted to see every bird in the book and so joined a small sub-group of the bird club generally known as 'twitchers' who tick off each bird on the list they have seen and will travel miles just to claim and photograph a rare visitor.

Fate had given a further turn to the screw.

He purchased an expensive camera complete with long range telephoto lenses, in this he was assisted by an extremely attractive, younger lady called Irene.

And there went fate twisting away again.

It was inevitable that with their mutual interest and being so often thrown into each other's company that Jim and Irene would become close friends. Irene was also married but as with Jim her spouse was not in the least bit interested in birds, his main pastime being drinking in which he indulged often and thoroughly.

They fell for each other.

But apart from an occasional awkward fumbling kiss when out of sight from the other twitchers they could only tell each other what they would like to do if the opportunity arose. Jim was at first shocked then aroused by the nature of the activities suggested by Irene.

They agreed that they would if they could, when Jim had a bright idea - the plan was the most natural of all and was fool proof

Now it is well known in engineering circles that a fool proof plan is proof of a fool.

But it was an excellent plan.

Whilst twitching they had come across a nice hollow in the ground way out on the moors comfortably padded with soft heather and a long way from anywhere. The spot was ideal and they agreed on a day and time they would meet there approaching from quite different directions.

The way in which the twitcher's world works is that should a rare species be identified by a member of the group other members would be phoned and its wherabouts passed on so that they might jump in their cars and head for the spot before the bird saw fit to move on having realised that Ilkley Moor was not Brittany.

So all they had to do was to phone each other up to advise that a blue throated robin had been seen on the appropriate moor and was not likely to be there for long.

Both their partners were used to such messages and the subsequent rush for clothing and equipment followed by a dash for the car and a hurried goodbye.

When the day arrived all went as arranged and no suspicions were aroused in either home.

As it happened it was a beautiful warm sunny day. The moors were a carpet of purple heather; the air was soft and crystal clear from yesterday's rain now dried off in the heat of mid-day.

They found the hollow and each other.

The rush of pent-up passion was slowed by their lack of experience of each other, and they were determined to make the loving last as long as possible. Jim was entranced as Irene's body was revealed, and she was excited by Jim's thoughtful handling, a pleasant contrast to her husband's drunken attempts at seduction.

It was therefore some considerable time before they lay exhausted in each other's arms and then they dozed satisfied in the warmth of the afternoon.

Jim had no idea how long he had been asleep, but he was suddenly brought wide awake by a quite loud 'CLICK'. He quickly disentangled himself and sat up. What he saw made his blood turn to ice in his veins. He was looking directly into a telephoto lens attached to a camera behind which he could distinguish the face of a well known club member.

As Irene tried to cover her nakedness they became aware of the others, it seemed that nearly all the club were there with a battery of cameras all busy recording the scene. As they scrambled to dress a ragged cheer went up from the assembled throng which then dispersed chuckling, giggling and outright laughing.

***

Jim's wife and Irene's husband never understood why their partners suddenly and with no convincing reason left the bird club. And life settled back to its previous pace. But as these things happen the Autumn copy of the bird club magazine still to its original distribution list arrived at each house and was opened out of curiosity by each spouse. The centre pages were given over to a picture of a blue throated robin taken by a moorland hollow. There in the background could barely be seen a pair of entangled naked human forms. Their faces were indistinguishable but on the grass Jim's wife could make out Jim's unique jacket, and Irene's unusual flowery dress.

JML
4/7/2005

⸙ **HE SOLD EVERYTHING** ⸘

*I*t was late December and dark when Phillip Gambon awoke in Scotland. Yesterday had been a great success, at least by his sales targets all of which he had exceeded. Phillip liked selling and considered himself to be one of the company's best, consistently out-selling his competitors. At forty-five he thought himself to be the natural choice to take his manager's position as boss of the outfit's national sales force.

And he was keen and ambitious, very ambitious.

As he tucked into the very large all English breakfast, he contemplated yet again the competition to his promotion. It appeared to him that there was little to be feared from the men on the team as all but one of them were relatively young, inexperienced, and easily distracted, and the only other was long in the tooth and looking forward to an early retirement.

The real problem was the only female member of the group. Unmarried and reasonably attractive in a severe, standoffish, way, she was as determined as he was on success. In fact Gloria Standish was a considerable hit with higher management, understood the company politics, and being of a similar age to himself also regularly produced sales figures on target.

In addition, due to an early misunderstanding - she had mistaken his friendliness for something more and when he made his lack of interest clear she had turned against him, and took every opportunity to score off him. To suggest they disliked each other was an understatement.

He was however convinced that he would win the race.

Setting these negative thoughts aside he studied the map to select the easiest and fastest route south.

His boss had called for a team meeting. This was planned to start at two p.m., and because his boss was a keen walker it was to be held at a small but good hotel in a little village in the Lake District. As accommodation out of season was scarce the team were distributed around several bed and breakfast establishments in the locality.

Time was not on his side as he would need to leave well before dawn the following day in order to reach his next client in good order.

Having settled his account he was soon on his way and as the car warmed to a comfortable temperature and he slotted into the south-bound traffic his thoughts turned to the day's prospects. The meeting was unlikely to present any problems, his manager would no doubt congratulate him on yesterday's success, and as far as he knew there were no company problems in sight.

He was very much looking forward to the evening and night. His wife Angie was visiting one of her many ancient aunties in the Lakes and had promised to join him for his overnight stay, she was to return home the next day, whilst he would set off early meet to his client in Wales. To this end he had asked his boss's secretary to book a double room at his allotted B & B. Excited at this prospect - he loved his wife, and loved these off the cuff meetings away from home. These and many like thoughts eased the drive as the miles rolled past under his wheels.

But fate was not due to be that kind.

It would take him in its most unforgiving grip and not let go.

Its first sign was untroubling - the traffic gradually slowed to a halt. A relaxed Phillip sat back and waited patiently for things to get moving again as they invariably did.

However after ten minutes he began to feel some concern. At fifteen minutes he realised there was no traffic in the opposite direction, and the driver of the car in front was walking back towards him. As a result of their discussion Phillip turned his radio to the station they agreed might provide the best traffic news.

Then. 'We are just getting news of a serious traffic accident on the main north-south route a few miles north of the Scottish border.' The radio said.

'We will keep you up-dated as news comes in.'

This was followed minutes later by a police car whose loud hailer was commanding -.

"There has been a major road accident - stay where you are, do not attempt to turn round as the opposite carriageway is required for rescue vehicles. Thank you."

Well, for Phillip this was a disaster. As an ambulance with siren blasting roared past he knew he would not make the meeting.

His first move was to pull out his mobile phone to contact his boss, but all he managed in that person's absence was to leave a message with the secretary, very much aware of how weak an excuse it sounded. He did however manage to convey the gist of yesterday's success.

At this stage he felt sure that he would at least be in time to have dinner with his wife.

Several hours later, still stuck, with police, fire engines, and ambulance passing frequently the size of the problem was making itself clear. The radio was reporting it as the worst road disaster for many years.

As dusk arrived Phillip in despair phoned his allotted B & B whose phone number he had obtained from the secretary.

The proprietor was sympathetic and agreed to leave the side door on the latch and also promised to leave some food and a bottle of whiskey out for him, and he would see him in the morning.

But he then failed to contact his wife either on the home phone or her mobile.

It was after one a.m. when a very miserable and tired Phillip let himself in to an unfamiliar B & B, found his way to the Lounge and by the gentle light of a standard lamp sat down to the sandwiches and whiskey that had been left for him.

Suddenly relaxed he enjoyed several large whiskies whose effect on him became clear when he finally stood up to take himself to bed.

And here a small difficulty arose - he had no idea which room his wife was in.

The register, if it existed, was nowhere to be found, so in a somewhat befuddled state he made his way upstairs and contemplated the row of closed doors that confronted him.

Much, much later he realised that a wiser or more sober man would have retired downstairs to sleep on the lounge sofa; but he felt in a wooley way that fate now owed him a night with his lawful wife, and he would have this at all cost.

There was a light showing under the first door and he felt that by now she would be asleep, so this one he ignored.

The next was locked.

As he turned the handle of the next a definitely male voice told him to bugger off.

He gently opened the next and final door, peered into the gloom and was rewarded by the welcome sight of a female form asleep in a big double bed.

Phillip was home and dry.

He quietly undressed and climbed in beside the recumbent figure, at the same time recognising that very familiar perfume.

A while later he passed his arm around her and half awake and half asleep they made soft, gentle, and relaxing love.

Long before dawn Phillip slid out of bed, grabbed his clothes and so as not to awake his partner made his way to the bathroom where he washed and dressed.

The proprietor was just putting the finishing touches to the breakfast preparations, and on his own Phillip ate, paid his bill and left a note for the lady in room four, which simply said 'Thank you love' and was signed with their private symbol of affection which was three kisses in the shape of a star.

Then a much happier Phillip was on his way through Lakeland's wonderful scenery on golden breaking dawn to his welsh client and the prospect of more sales in mind.

He felt good. But fate knew better.

The Welsh client was happy to provide him with a satisfyingly large order and by mid afternoon he was on his way home and a discussion of the recent events with his wife.

Dusk was slowly swallowing the scenery as he turned his car into their neat drive, parked, and slowly savouring the moment walked the few remaining paces to the front door. With a terrific sense of relief he turned the key in the lock and entered into that familiar and welcoming environment they called home.

His wife was busy in the kitchen, and his heart gladdened as it always did when he saw her. His romantic feelings for her had in no way lessened with the passing of the years since they had met and instantly fallen in love.

She turned and with her hands in the bowl of flour she leaned forward and kissed him.

The next moment he would never ever forget.

'I'm awfully sorry I couldn't make it yesterday,' she said.

'Only our neighbour was suddenly taken to hospital and I stayed with her to make sure she was OK. The battery of my mobile was flat; I hope you got the message I left with the secretary?'

Phillip felt his blood turn to ice in his veins.

A cold hand grabbed his heart and squeezed it and he could not breath.

Fortunately his wife had returned her attention to the bowl and did not see the expression of anguish that Phillip did his best to hide.

He excused himself, hurriedly left his wife, poured himself a very stiff drink and considered his dilemma.

After worrying himself for some time he concluded that he had unwittingly made love to a complete stranger. His wife had no inkling of this, and, he felt there was little or no chance of her ever finding out. As the episode was not of his making he felt that his conscience was clear and resolved to forget the whole thing.

But fate had her teeth into him and was not about to let go.

It was a struggle, but he was able to cheer his wife with his selling successes and the evening passed off without her noticing anything amiss. Pleading tiredness he went to bed and slept

***

The following day, and in a much more relaxed frame of mind Phillip drove to the office, even giggling to himself as his memory stirred with pictures of his little adventure. He felt safe.

(Did we hear fate give a chuckle?)

To his surprise his boss called him in to his office as soon as he arrived, and did not wait to hear of his successes.

'Come in. Shut the door.'

'Sit down.'

Pause

'I have been promoted.'

And without waiting for Phillip's congratulations, continued.

'My old position is therefore vacant, and I'm sorry but you're not going to like this, Gloria Standish will be taking over. I wanted you, but management insisted - this is what the meeting in the Lakes was all about.'

'I'm Sorry......................'

A very downcast Phillip left his boss. As he trudged in misery along the passage he passed a partially open door through which he could hear Gloria Standish's easily recognised voice.

'...............and I have no idea who he was, but he made love beautifully and even left a note signed with a star.'

Then it dawned on Phillip - so that was the familiar perfume.

He left the office, left the building, and left the firm, for ever.

JML
13/8/2005

CHIMERA

For some time, ever since their fortieth birthdays (they were within a few days of each other), Reginald and Elouise Tops had gradually become aware that something was not as it once was. Almost imperceptibly at first it grew slowly until after some considerable time it began to affect their lives.

They both held down professional well paid and pensionable jobs, had a car each, a beautiful well organised home and many good and cherished friends.

There had only ever been the two of them and since meeting for the first time as teenagers they had been in love with each other. Deeply attached - they were considerably jealous of this close relationship and nothing was allowed to disturb it.

So what then was going wrong?

Reggie was still attending the gym, had avoided mid life podginess, and kept himself in good condition for his wife. A naturally attractive man he kept himself to himself in spite of the ready attentions of the opposite sex. Elouise, it could be said, was even more pleasing to look at. No child birth had spoilt her very obviously feminine figure; and she also took great pride in looking her best - not for men in general - but for her Reggie.

So what then was going wrong?

Their love life had always been important to them both, and they felt that it was the cornerstone of their relationship. Always ready to discuss it and improve it they had for some time indulged in experimentation. Willing to try something new, they had purchased books and video tapes of all kinds and each had worked hard to give maximum pleasure to the other. And this very fundamental aspect of life they enjoyed very much indeed.

So what then was going wrong?

Well, having tried every exciting variation they could think of between two people of the opposite sex, and this many times, it was dawning on each of them that their lovemaking was starting to be a bit boring. They began to know in advance what to expect - there were no more surprises.

Round about their forty-fifth birthday they realised that their usual eagerness to make love was on the wane. On the odd occasion it was avoided by the flimsiest of excuses (by both parties). This was rare at first but eventually became quite usual.

The glue which held them together was slowly coming unstuck. And month by month it was becoming more obvious.

Unfortunately neither of them had developed wider interests preferring instead to simply enjoy each other. However he made an attempt to offset the problem (as now they agreed it was) by joining the local golf club, but soon found that he lacked all aptitude with the clubs themselves.

Similarly Elouise found that the ladies circle was not her cup of tea, or in their case glass of sherry.

So, it soon became a routine topic of conversation between them, and occasionally they would fall into the trap of blaming each other.

'I feel that you're not enjoying it any more.' This from Reggie.

'Well perhaps it doesn't excite me like it used to - and you keep falling asleep.' Responds Elouise.

'It seems ages since we made love out of doors, you used to think that was terrific.' Complains Reggie.

'That's because you always choose unsuitable places - like last time when we were just the other side of a hedge from a walker's path with giggling scouts and guides peeking at us,' Elouise responds, 'and it was bloody uncomfortable, I couldn't sit down for a week.'

Then one day a small thing happened which was to change everything.

Reggie watched a TV program about lesbians.

At first he was simply intrigued, engrossed as he was in love between members of the opposite sex this aspect of loving had escaped his attention. But after the programme he found himself thinking about it more and more, and from intrigue his thoughts changed to fascination and then excitement. He started to form mental pictures of Elouise making love with another woman and soon found that this gave him a thrill he had not felt for a very long time.

Eventually he decided that with nothing to loose he would like to involve Elouise, at least in considering a lesbian lover.

To this end he selected some video tapes of loving females all of which had nothing but attractive subjects.

These he enjoyed on his own for some time before he introduced them to Elouise.

On this occasion he was only interested in Elouise's reaction, and it surprised and puzzled him - he had expected expressions of horror and disgust followed by outright rejection and her walking out before the tape ended.

Instead she sat silent and still throughout the whole tape and afterwards was quiet and very thoughtful, saying shyly that she wouldn't mind seeing it again sometime.

And Reggie obliged.

Eventually Elouise let Reggie know that the lesbian idea excited her and that she had often dreamed of what it might be like to love another woman.

After much discussion they agreed to try this within certain rules. These were:

1. Reggie was not interested in man with man situations.
2. He would not tolerate Elouise going with another man, women only.
3. He would not be present so as to allow her complete freedom of action.
4. He would approve her selection.
5. It would not be permanent (a one off only was proposed).
6. And she would tell him all about it afterwards.

Now Reggie knew from discussions with his work colleagues of a club in town where, it was said, people with all kinds of deviations met, danced, drank and made associations.

So on one fateful evening, with Elouise dressed to kill, they set off for the club.

It was as they had described it.

Homosexuals of both kinds, transvestites, boy/girls and girl/boys, old and young, they were all there.

They bought drinks, separated, and after some time Reggie saw that Elouise had not only picked a girl but was dancing with her, and he was astonished, and to his surprise found himself somewhat hurt and not a little jealous.

The girl was stunning.

Long blond hair framed smiling eyes that complimented a model's features. Her figure was soft and beautifully femininely rounded. The whole effect was temptingly seductive. She and Elouise were quite the most attractive pair in the place and were collecting many an admiring glance.

Much later, back home, Elouise let Reggie know that she found Sam, for that was the girl's name, very attractive and that she might, if Sam were willing, like to spend a night with her.

And so the die was cast.

Elouise went to the club on her own, as she complained that Reggie was inhibiting her actions, and after a few such evenings reported to Regie that a night together had been arranged, and this in due course took place.

As the date for the assignation approached they both for quite different reasons found themselves engulfed by a mounting excitement.

On the appointed night Reggie on his own in the local hotel found sleep impossible, his mind a turmoil of lustful imaginings mixed with envy and not a little hurt.

However he had convinced himself that this would bring them closer again, and was impatient to hear in detail how they had made love. He was after all well aware that Elouise might want to make the new liaison permanent.

It was the following evening when Reggie and Elouise were finally re-united - and for Reggie the occasion was a shock. Nothing was as he had imagined it would be.

Instead of Elouise being all of a glow as she was after love making and being eager to tell him all about it, she was pale and withdrawn and reluctant to bring the subject up. Rather than telling Regie in detail what had taken place she merely said, 'It was OK.' and refused to enlarge on this all too brief statement.

After several attempts to get her to say more Reggie simply assumed it had not worked out. Elouise made it plain she would never again even consider repeating the experience, and so he decided that was the end of that.

But that was not the end of that.

Having put his wife's adventure behind him, he found that he could not get the memory of Sam out of his mind.

At first he thought it was just because as a lesbian she was a novelty to him, but he soon began to recognise that he was smitten by her sheer sexiness. He could not let go of what was becoming a deep longing for her. Her image would appear in his mind at the most discomforting times, and these occasions were becoming ever more frequent and insistent. He started to wonder what Sam was really like to talk to, to hold, to make love to.

Reggie also felt strongly that he had been cheated by Elouise in that by not describing to him her experience with Sam she had broken their agreement.

It was this latter consideration that finally freed him to make the next fatal move.

And so, without telling Elouise, he went back to the club and after fighting a loosing battle with his conscience picked up the courage to speak to Sam. He found that everything about her excited him, this lovely girl could not only hold a sensible conversation but oozed sexual attraction. In addition to these deepening feelings, as he saw more of Sam he began to feel that his attraction for her was returned.

Reggie was smitten. Head over heels smitten. Lost.

He also thought that if he got to know Sam better he might find out what had taken place between her and Elouise.

And so it was that several visits to the club later he persuaded Sam to spend a night with him. Sam of course was unaware of his relationship with Elouise and Reggie was determined to keep it so.

His job occasionally took him to parts of the country where he had to stay overnight and it was on one of these visits he persuaded Sam to join him at his hotel. And so it was arranged.

Reggie could hardly wait, and erotic thoughts of the lovely Sam constantly filled his mind. But eventually the day came. He met Sam in the bar and after drinks and a leisurely meal they retired to his room.

***

Nervous at first he kissed Sam and slowly they began to exchange caresses.

It was when Reggie started to feel below Sam's waist that he realised with a dreadful shock of anguish and horror that froze the blood in his veins and made his skin crawl with dread, what a terrible mistake he had made.

That night he slept in his car, and in the morning left without seeing Sam.

The lesbian episode was never again mentioned between Reggie and his spouse. Their love making became less frequent and they drifted into old age where excuses became the norm, and Reggie destroyed the tapes.

JML
24/8/2005

⇜ **THE FARM** ⇝

*J*oe and Rachel Blackson ran Hollowend Farm very well indeed. Not only did it pay them both a handsome income but it also made a reasonable profit.

This was mainly due to Rachel who loved it and spent every moment of every long day hard at work nurturing its live stock and tending its broad green fields. She had always loved it ever since helping out as a small child and later as a teenager.

She married Joe to be on the farm; no love match this; more one of mutual need - he needed a wife, she the farm.

Joe did not like the farm much, he preferred to be down at the village pub instead of grubbing about in the muck, and he was permanently angry with Rachel for not providing him with a son to hand the farm on to.

Rachel was happy and always busy, but she had one problem in the shape of Joe's younger brother Seb. Seb also preferred to be down at the local but he fancied Rachel something rotten, and would turn up with the excuse of helping out when he knew Joe to be away. On these occasions he would follow Rachel about and seize any slight opportunity to grab her very comely figure - an event that Rachel detested and always had a farm tool handy with which to discourage further advances. Complaints to Joe had no effect, their love making had long since passed into history, and he was fond of Seb.

Rachel was used to the situation, and tolerated the brothers for the sake of the farm.

She knew all the livestock by name, talked to each of them every day, and wept when they were taken away to be slaughtered. On these occasions she felt like a traitor.

The fields drew her and she was never happier than when sitting high on the big tractor, hauling one of the many pieces of machinery in circles or strips, with only the wind, clouds, sun and earth for company except for one of their border collies.

In fact she was part of the farm and the farm knew it and responded.

Life was good and at thirty she looked and felt healthy and attractive. The farm was enough and she was content.

All on the farm was well, and the annual routine ran its course year by year.

Until Joe died.

Rachel knew that Joe had a serious heart condition as had his brother which they had inherited from their father. But Joe had taken life easy for some time and had shown no sign of his imminent demise.

But suddenly there he was - dead.

It fell to Rachel to make all the funeral arrangements and it was a success. Joe was popular in the village, the church was full and most came back to the farm where they enjoyed a farm style meal and drinks. Many a mourner had to walk home somewhat the worse for the booze. Joe had a very convivial send off, but the next day the farm made its demands and from dawn onwards Rachel was back into the routine. She did not mourn - there was simply no time.

It was therefore a week later when she got a call from the local solicitor to arrange for the reading of Joe's will.

Rachel had no suspicion of anything untoward, and had no inkling of the shock that was about to befall.

The first indication that anything was wrong was when the solicitor insisted that Joe's brother Seb must also be present.

And so the three of them found themselves comfortably seated in the farm sitting room with Seb lounging in an easy chair and Rachel and the solicitor upright and attentive at the big oak table.

At first the only sound was the lazy crackle of the wood fire; then he began.

'Joe,' he said, 'recognised that Rachel was part of the farm and that it would be useless without her.'

Rachel smiled, but the solicitor looked very unhappy.

'Therefore,' he continued, 'he has left the farm to Seb but only on the condition that he marries Rachel.'

This was greeted by a stunned silence.

Seb swore, although he was attracted by his late brother's wife he was used to a single existence and the last thing he wanted was a wife's nagging.

Rachel was distraught, bewildered, hurt; feelings that were soon replaced by anger and disbelief.

The recipients broke the silence together.

Seb - 'What the bloody hell, who does he think he is, the miserable bugger. If he wasn't dead I'd kill the sod.'

Rachel - 'There must be a mistake. Is it a joke? Can he do this?'

A most unhappy solicitor told them that not only could he do this but that it was all legal and above board.

Then -

'The will gives you three months to be wed otherwise the farm goes up for auction and the proceeds will go to Joe and Seb's cousin Daniel in Australia.'

Seb swore again.

Rachel said nothing.

The solicitor said he was sorry and left the bewildered pair.

Seb left still swearing, and it was several days before either Rachel or Seb could bring themselves to discuss the awful situation in which they found themselves.

In the meantime Rachel had realised that without the farm her life was without meaning and she would do anything to remain part of it. And Seb had realised that without his brother's regular and generous handouts he would need the income from the farm to survive.

So they agreed to meet.

Wary of each other, and suspicious they sat uncomfortably on opposite sides of the table were just a short while before the solicitor had read them Joe's ultimatum.

'Well, aint this just a bugger?' Seb's opener was a statement not a question.

'A right bugger.' Rachel agreed.

A long thoughtful silence followed. Then-

'We don't seem to have much of a choice,' Rachel admitted resignedly. 'I am prepared to go through with it but there has to be rules.'

Seb's reaction was predictable. 'What the hell do you mean, rules?' He ground out.

'Well - You must let me manage the farm and give me help when I require it. You will only take out the same money as Joe did.' Here she paused, but Seb was listening intently.

'Separate bedrooms and no sex.'

Much to her surprise Seb seemed not to react. In fact he was beginning to realise that if he was to live the easy life he was used to he had no choice but to accept.

'Just one thing,' he said eventually, 'I must have overall financial control.'

'Only if you ensure the farm gets what it needs.' Rachel said with great reluctance. She also had concluded that she had no choice.

And so it was agreed and this reluctant bride and groom were quietly married, and Seb moved into the farm.

Now for some time everything went well. Rachel continued to run the farm with a grumbling Seb helping out when not attending several pints at the local.

But it couldn't last.

Seb wanted to play the squire and bought a big and very expensive car. He gained local favour by regularly treating the whole pub to a round of drinks.

It was rumoured that he had a young mistress in the local town - he certainly went there often enough.

He gambled much and mostly lost. And he was nearly always drunk by mid afternoon. At night he had once or twice tried Rachel's bedroom door but it was always locked. So much for wifely comforts he thought.

Rachel observed Seb's activities with growing concern, but tolerated the situation for the sake of the farm.

But then Seb having used up all of his agreed income started to make use of the funds needed to maintain the farm. This in spite of Rachel's protests which just made matters worse as Seb reacted to being criticised and promptly ate further into much needed funds.

Now to Rachel, it was essential to make hay whilst the sun shone. Profit gained from the sale of stock and crops had to be ploughed back in if they were to reap the benefits, and Seb's careless spending was seriously jeopardising the farm, and this hurt Rachel and a dreadful fear grew in her. Seb's loose living was affecting his health and he had a series of increasingly serious and very painful chest pains. In spite of the doctors warnings he continued to get worse. In fact he could no longer help out when needed which also hampered Rachel's ability to keep the farm running. It was now making a loss, and Rachel was at risk of loosing all she had ever wanted and lived for.

Something had to be done. And she had to do it.

So! One winter's night when Seb had returned from a bout of even for him excessively heavy drinking, and was helped upstairs to his bedroom by Rachel, she made her move.

Dressed in her most figure hugging nightgown she entered his room with a tray of food and a bottle of whisky. In spite of the drink she found him awake and reading a newspaper. At first she was shocked by his appearance, lying there he looked old and ill and for a second she nearly gave in, but the thought of the farm determined her and she steeled her will.

She placed the tray by the bed and leaned over and kissed him. She then stroked and teased him in every way short of sex as only a woman determined on seduction can.

Seb swallowed his amazement and struggled manfully to respond, but the more he tried the more Rachel teased.

Suddenly she saw the pain in his eyes and the skin of his face turned grey, sweat bathed his body and he was unable to speak.

Then Rachel calmly removed the tray, and as she left the room she moved his pills to the dressing table just out of his reach.

***

In the morning he was dead. The farm was saved.

The funeral was held, Seb's demise had been expected, and in due course the solicitor arrived to read Seb's will.

Rachel was disturbed when a most anxious solicitor was followed by an elderly man with much the look of Seb and his brother, and not a little worse for drink.

The solicitor introduced this person as Joe and Seb's cousin Dan from Australia.

'The Farm goes to Seb's cousin Daniel.' The solicitor pointed to the stranger. 'Only on the basis that he and Rachel Marry.' His words hung heavy in the air.

To say that Rachel was stunned was an understatement - how could this happen a second time - what on earth had she done to deserve such misfortune. She wept in despair.

But she soon discovered that Daniel had lost his farm in Australia which went bust, and that he was broke.

All of which he blamed on his 'dicky ticker' as he put it.

And so Rachel began to lay her plans, this time well in advance.

After all the farm must be saved. Mustn't it?

JML
23/9/2005

⸙ **THE VISIT** ⸙

We left Gerald Handle, you may remember, having won the National Lottery and having had his amazing, life changing, experience with 'the girls' at his farewell party.

He next decided to take his future by the scruff of the neck and shake it into life. He wanted to make something of himself that he could admire.

Firstly he sought a place to live where he could enjoy being part of the English countryside, so he purchased a sizable residence in its own grounds on the outskirts of one of our oldest university towns. He hired a gardener and a visiting daily cleaner so that the effort of running the place would be minimal.

Then he looked round at his elegant furnishings and strolled about his estate, and felt incredibly, depressingly and hollowly lonely.

After some time this emptiness forced him to seek company and even friendship. To this end he joined a very vigourous, noisy, and healthily cosmopolitan debating society. He ate out often and rejoiced in many a goodly pint in the local pub.

This went some way to satisfying his needs, but there was a gaping hole - love. He had none. He had proved himself locally popular but this was no substitute, and he had no idea how to solve his growing ache.

It was in the end resolved for him.

The next house along from his came up for sale and was soon taken by a woman, a single person like himself, or so it was rumoured locally.

'Go for it Gerry,' they said, 'she's a cracker. And wealthy.'

This last was obvious since one couldn't live there without having considerable financial resources.

But Gerald was, as ever, reluctant to push himself forward. It was therefore some time before they eventually met, and not in favourable circumstances.

She drove into the back of him at a set of traffic lights. He was uninjured but his car was considerably bent as was his self control.

'What the hell!' He shouted. 'Couldn't you see they were at red?'

She was contrite, offered to compensate him, and blamed the wet conditions for her lapse.

A week later Gerald found that try as he would he could not get his neighbour out of his mind. And soon it was every waking and sleeping minute. It did eventually dawn on him that in that short and unfortunate meeting he had fallen in love. Head over bloody heels in love. Desperately, totally, and bewilderingly in love, but he had no clue as to what to do about it. However his luck held and the problem, as before, was solved for him.

On a wonderfully fresh and sunshining day she drove up his drive knocked on his door and presented him with a cheque for the damage to his car.

That was the start of a wondrous courtship and they were married quietly in the university town and honeymooned in Bali. Sophie was everything Gerald could wish for.

Neither of them had living parents or any close relatives so the wedding guests were all local acquaintances and friends.

Life was kind to Gerald and Sophie and soon they were rewarded with two lovely children, one of each sex the girl being the elder.

But out of sight, over the horizon a black cloud was drifting slowly their way heavy with lightening about to strike.

This took the form of Grant Sedgewick one of Gerald's ex-work colleagues.

He knocked on their door having, he claimed, been visiting the village whilst on a holiday tour. Gerald politely asked him in and he readily accepted the large whiskey he was offered. Hesitant at first but then oiled by the drink he admitted that he had been made redundant and was currently looking for a job. Gerald was sympathetic but cautious.

Then Sophie entered and was introduced to Grant, and Grant's reaction puzzled Gerald - he could have sworn that Grant recognised Sophie but it was evident that this was not returned.

Their somewhat stilted conversation was interrupted by the noisy and happy entrance of the children. Soon after Grant took his leave after persuading Gerald to join him for a night out with dinner in town the following day.

'I don't know why but I took an instant dislike to your friend,' Sophie admitted, 'he is unhappy and envious of us.' She concluded.

'He is not my friend.' Gerald told her. 'We simply worked at the same place.'

'Then what was the purpose of his visit?'

'I have no idea,' Gerald admitted.

'I suspect he's after money.' She warned. 'Do be careful.'

Gerald had some time to consider the visitor's motives and before setting out for their meeting had concluded that Sophie may well be right; and he determined to stay sober and be on his guard.

They met, and it was during the meal that he sensed that Grant was wound up like a spring. In order to pre-empt a request for funds he explained to Grant that on winning the lottery he had been advised to turn down all and every request for loans or gifts, and this was his unswerving policy.

'I quite understand.' Grant ground out, and sat there silent and unmoving for some time.

Grant had drunk a fair amount by now, but Gerald ordered another bottle and topped up his companion's glass. Grant was evidently psyching himself up for something.

A something that was about to invade Gerald's comfortable world.

Then -

'I have to say something.' Grant's voice was barely audible and he leaned across the table, his face intent, his eyes boring into Gerald's.

'What do you know about your wife's past?' The words stabbed Gerald like a knife.

'Not a great deal before she arrived here.' He admitted, 'Why?'

With hardly hidden satisfaction Grant told his tale, and as he did Gerald's heart knew a pain he had never before felt.

Grant had recognised Sophie as a girl who lived near Grant in one of London's suburbs.

'She lived alone,' he said, 'and with no regular job, yet she had become quite wealthy. She was well known to be a high class call girl.'

Having delivered his bombshell, Grant leaned back to watch the effect of the bitter revelation on Gerald, and was rewarded with a picture of anguish and disbelief.

Gerald's mind was in a whirl, dazed and distraught he paid the bill and assassin and victim left the restaurant.

'Never mind old chap, I know a place where you can get your own back.' Grant said as he pushed Gerald into a waiting taxi.

A bewildered Gerald had little idea what Grant was talking about and had completely lost all will of independent action. He slumped down in his seat and tried to grasp what it all meant.

The taxi took them to a street in town that Gerald did not recognise. Grant paid the cabby and bundled Gerald up some steps and after ringing the bell the door opened and they were immediately welcomed inside by a woman large in every sense.

Still not clear what was happening to him Gerald found himself alone in a room with a bed on which lounged a girl dressed in what was obviously night attire. Nonplussed Gerald close to tears sagged onto the end of the bed. The girl greeted him in a friendly way as she realised that here something was terribly wrong.

'Want to tell me about it dear?' She said. 'You look terrible.'

'No.' Gerald managed. 'Just let me sit for a while.'

'I'm afraid it will cost you just the same.' The girl said not unsympathetically.

At which Gerald drew out his wallet and gave the girl a pile of notes which when she had counted them was three times what she would have asked him for. She was concerned at his distress but was worldly wise enough to be silent.

Eventually and after only a few minutes Gerald thanked the girl, found his way out into the deserted street and started to walk.

He walked and walked along streets he had never seen, and as he did his mind started to clear, and he began to take a grip of his situation.

One thing became paramount - Sophie must know nothing of what had taken place. Having determined this he found a taxi and was soon at his own front door. With the familiarity of his home came calm and as his world wrapped him in its cocoon, he was almost convinced the awful revelation had not happened.

The next day and for some time Gerald was on tenterhooks in case Grant turned up again to cause more mischief but he heard nothing of him. He said nothing to Sophie of what Grant had told him.

Then a strange thing happened.

Grant had left his card on his visit and unknown to Gerald, Sophie ranking him as a friend of Gerald's added him to their Christmas card list. And so, come Christmas as it was Sophie who did the cards, a card, which had their address in fancy print, was duly dispatched.

***

Early in that New Year a letter arrived from a neighbour and friend of Grant's. He said he was sorry to have to tell them that Grant had some time ago been diagnosed as having Aids, but he had refused to acknowledge the fact. He had refused all treatment and medication, and with the resulting loss of immunity, had contracted pneumonia. He had died quietly on Christmas day. Details of the funeral were included but the date had passed.

Gerald never did tell Sophie what he had been told, and through the rest of their long, happy, and very busy life together he quite forgot that it had ever taken place.

JML
30/9/2005

❦ **BACK FROM THE BRINK** ❧

*I*f making love is the chemistry that binds couples together, then Jack and Julie had mislaid the formula.

The successful bringing up of their four gifted children had, together with his full and her part time jobs, occupied all their available space night and day. They had done well, and considered themselves to have made a good fist of life - but now they were heading for disaster.

Jack was now retired from a very busy city job, Julie had at last given up her occasional work, and some months back their youngest, the last, had left home attracted by a very well paid job abroad. And now the strain of finding themselves continually alone together for the first time since their honeymoon all those years ago was beginning to tell.

It was not so much the arguments that sprang up from nowhere appearing out of the most trivial event, it was the complete lack of interest shown by both parties in each other in the physical side things.

Some force that once was there was now missing.

The future began to seem bleak indeed to both of them.

And yet they were not old, they had maintained their general health and as yet showed none of the tell tale signs of old age. Amongst their friends they were each considered to be good looking, and when in company received many an admiring glance.

What made matters worse was that they each considered the other to be responsible for the problem, mentally disowning blame for the lack of physical contact.

In truth they were both in part equally to blame.

The situation had grown up slowly and insidiously over the years, almost un-noticed at first, and subsequently treated as temporary, with many an all too reasonable excuse. Eventually temporary became permanent.

Let it be said that it was in no way that their desires had lessened. They each found others physically desirable and dreamed often of clandestine relationships.

Jack especially was affected by this lack of spice in his life, he felt that he was looking into a pool of emptiness which was deepening year by year and into which he was permanently on the edge of drowning. Julie was better off in that as a woman she could always loose herself in the minutia of keeping their house fit for visitors, and maintaining contact with the children.

The routine of life was however regularly lifted out of monotony by their lifelong friends Bill and Belinda.

Now 'The Bees' as Bill and Belinda were fondly known by 'The Jays' had in the past made matters worse by giving many a broad hint as to their active and enjoyable sex life. But as the friendship lengthened they came to understand that all was not well with the Jays in this department and learned to treat the matter as a bit of a joke. They were in fact supremely envious of that which the Jays had achieved, being somewhat less well off themselves.

Eventually they determined to interfere. Their plan hatched with the very worst intentions was however ill-conceived, risky, and ultimately changed the Jay's lives for ever.

They began by inviting the friends out for separate evenings on a man to man and woman to woman basis using the pretext of sharing a different range of interests.

We will follow Jack's progress to the final crisis, but that of his wife was similar.

To gain Jack's full confidence Bill introduced Jack to his gardening club and got him onto the pub darts team where to his surprise he became quite an asset showing real talent at chucking the 'arrers'.

Julie was only too pleased to escape from mere domesticity by joining Belinda's book and film group, and both took to having frequent meals out he with him and she with her, thus they established completely separate existences. The fact that the Bees stayed together at all was a source of comment and astonishment to the very jealous Jays.

Now into this volatile situation the Bees threw a match.

They acted with the worst of intentions and the results were......, well we shall see.

When Jack had indulged in slightly more than his usual modest alcohol intake at one of their man to man evenings out Bill began the process that he and Belinda had agreed. He started by casually mentioning that they had met a very attractive lady with whom they were keen to make friends.

But in spite of Jack's polite questions of interest Bill would not be drawn further on the matter and the subject of the new lady friend was neatly replaced by the latest political scandal. But the bait had been presented.

At their next assignment Bill again mentioned the mysterious lady adding that she seemed to them to be very sexy, and as such was always seductively attired. More than this Bill declined to say pleading ignorance.

As time went on Bill added more and more information about their new female friend, all of which was designed to encourage Jack's interest - and it did.

'Come on Bill give us all the gen. How old is she? Is she married? If not does she have a man in tow?' In spite of himself Jack could not let the matter rest.

'Where does she live? Does she work? Where does she spend her time?'

Bill was reticent.

'Come on Jack, you're a married man remember.'

But Bill made sure that Jack kept nibbling at the bait whilst keeping him from seeing the barbed hook it hid.

Then after several weeks Bill said casually, 'Why don't you come over to our place when our new friend is visiting and meet her for yourself?.'

Jack hesitated. Then -

'No I meant just me and her.'

They stared at each other neither daring to speak. Bill appalled at how successful their stratagem had been, how easily Jack had fallen in with it. Jack was shaken, he had said the words without really thinking and was surprised by his desire. He was also horrified by what Bill must think of him. He was at a loss for words.

'Er, I mean, I don't mean, ...'

'Don't worry old boy I won't say anything about this to the girls. And why shouldn't you get to meet her. There's no harm in looking, after all I have.'

Bill grinned lasciviously at this. Jack felt uncomfortable as if everyone was looking at him.

After a pause to let Jack recover, Bill said, 'It can easily be arranged, I can set it up for you if you would like, After that it would be up to you.'

On the brink Jack hesitated, he needed time to think, and with an effort changed the subject.

A month or so passed before the lady was again mentioned, during which Jack had mentally accepted Bill's proposition with an excitement that churned his insides, and rejected it with a feeling of relief.

But the anticipation and his imagination won, as Bill guessed it would. And so at their next lad's night out Jack tentativly and with pretended nonchalance asked if Bill had seen their new lady friend lately.

At this Bill was only too happy to supply Jack with details and much exaggerated descriptions of the lady's terrific good looks stressing their sexy nature.

'If ever there was a woman looking for love and ripe for it, it's she.' He stated, grinning knowingly.

And Jack swallowed the bait.

'I wouldn't mind just a look,' he said, 'it can't do any harm.'

Bill gloated but hid it well, and so they discussed how a meeting might be arranged. Jack swore Bill to secrecy.

About this time Belinda had agreed to make arrangements for Julie to meet their new man friend.

And thus the plan began to enfold with its inevitable consequences for the Jays.

Now plans are merely human things and are well known to be subject to the Umpty-jiggley of fate - and in this case the Umpty-jiggley was working overtime.

All (in human terms) was set, and Jack was to take one of the men's night out and instead he would attend the bar at a nearby rather posh hotel where the lady would be there to meet him, after which it was up to him.

Julie was scheduled to be out with Belinda as usual.

All dressed up for the occasion feeling nervous and something of a fool, Jack parked his car and made his way to the bar. He had a red rose in his lapel as an identifier as he expected did the lady.

But fate had Umpty-jiggled a great deal.

As Jack entered the bar area he immediately spotted the extremely attractive lady with a rose pinned to her dress - but what he saw took his breath away and made him stop shaking in his tracks.

For he recognised the lady.

It was his own wife.

With an effort he pulled himself together and made a bee-line for the gents where he found a cubicle, locked himself in, and tried to control his racing emotions.

His first thought was had she seen him, and felt some relief in thinking that she hadn't.

His second thought was what the hell was Bill playing at? He eventually concluded that it must be the Bees' clumsy attempt to bring them together.

Then he was nearly overwhelmed by the realisation of why he was there and shame filled his heart and with it came a sense of hopelessness.

But his final, surprising, and commanding thought was that he had never seen Julie look so inviting and that his love for her was suddenly the only thing that mattered, he felt he was loosing the power of rational thought, and as if in a dream he let himself out desperate to get to Julie before she vanished.

To his relief she was there having in fact seen him and gone through an identical set of thoughts she was waiting to see what Jack would do.

It was to Jack as if Julie was the unknown stranger and he approached quite shyly, and with a funny feeling in his throat said a soft 'good evening' and asked her if she would like a drink.

'I'd love one,' she said.

They played at being strangers. Jack ordered a table for two for dinner, and over the meal these two virtual strangers began to know each other. Their conversation never lagged they had so much to say. Years of misunderstanding and reticence were swept aside. After dinner and during an intimate nightcap Jack booked a room for the night.

And their loving captured all their pent-up longing. Afterwards they held each other close and talked with a love and honesty they had not known for a long time.

***

In a quite different Hotel across town a man and a woman each with a red rose met for the first time, liked each other, fell in love and without asking too many questions as to how they came to meet, a few weeks later became engaged and were eventually married.

The Umpty-jiggley had confused the meeting arrangements and because the Bees hadn't checked with each other they had scheduled both meetings for the same night. Then as a final act the Umpty-jiggley mixed up the hotels.

The Bees never found out what had actually taken place and were for ever puzzled by the generous reaction of both parties to their ill-intentioned plan.

JML
27/10/2005

❦ **PAST REGRETS** ❧

*I*t was May and the English Lake District displayed one of its rare perfect days. After breakfast the sun was high in the sky and the promised heat was gentled by a playful breeze which danced the outermost leaves on the trees. A day for the high fells if ever there was one.

He didn't know it but this one day was to throw its shadow over the rest of Kenneth Trendy's life.

At twenty three he was fit and eager to set off on his third day's walking of a well earned week's leave from his business.

With the intention of taking the path along Eskdale into the upper Esk and from there the little used path to Three Tarns and Bowfell and returning along the central ridge via Ore Gap, a damn good day's walk he reckoned.

He found the path along Eskdale by the river was deserted of people which was much as he preferred it. A hunting Kestrel was his only companion as he strode the length of the valley. And on and up he went gaining the haws at Three Tarns before he saw another person. As expected there were a few walkers on Bowfell summit but it has a wide top and he was able to lunch in an isolated spot with superb views along the length of Langdale.

Ken now had plenty of time to descend and he used it well stopping often to gaze in wonder as the scenes unfolded. The sun was still looking down through a clear sky and as the early breeze had dropped it was very warm.

In upper Esk the beck tumbled over a series of small waterfalls into clear pools as it made its chuckling way down hill. One of these pools was known to Ken from previous visits and he was now looking forward to assuaging the heat with a quick dip.

It was this simple act that brought sadness and grief to his whole life.

He reached the pool and after checking he was alone he stripped, jumped in, and relaxed as the cool water closed around him and started to ease his aching body.

Had he then left the pool and gone on his way all would have been well but he stayed: after all he was enjoying himself.

Then it happened.

Time from now on would stand still for Ken and every detail would be etched on his memory for all time.

It began innocently enough with a small shadow falling across the pool.

Ken looked up and was startled to see a girl standing looking down at him - with her back to the sun he could not see her expression. He thought that when she realised he was naked she would shy away and leave him to his pool.

But this did not happen.

Instead she said 'Hallo', and sat down.

'Is it cold?' She asked.

Peeved at being spied on, nevertheless Ken's good manners did not desert him.

'No,' he said, 'it's rather nice.'

What happened next startled and astonished him. The girl started to get undressed. No bra and pants occasion this she stood on the edge of the pool gloriously and beautifully naked.

And then she jumped in.

Now the pool was not large, it was in fact just about big enough for two people to stretch out without touching but not very much more. So it was impossible for these two to ignore each other, although at first Ken tried. But his attempts to hide himself and not study the girl gradually faded as she made no reservations in her open admiration of Ken.

She was bronzed all over and her sheer beauty soon created its physical reaction in Ken. Accidental touching became purposeful and Ken was encouraged by her ready laughter and easy smile to put his arms around her. To his surprise she kissed him, not a peck but a proper lover's kiss.

He helped her out onto the bank and then and there they made love long and complete in the soft sweet scented grass.

When at last they had little energy left for more they lay quiescent warmed by the late afternoon sun. And to Ken's lifelong regret he fell into a long, restful and dreamless sleep.

On awaking his first action was to turn to look at the girl.

She was gone.

Panic thoughts raced through his mind, had he merely dreamt it, was she close by but out of sight, was she playing games with him, had she really just upped and gone? It seemed to Ken incredible that after what had taken place she had simply and completely deserted him.

He looked for a note - none was there.

He felt hurt, let down, sad, angry, disappointed, stabbed to his heart, lost, bewildered. This was new territory for him and he was coming slowly to realise that the lost girl meant more to him than just a passing fling. He was falling in love with a memory. Deeply, totally, consumingly, and helplessly in love.

Eventually he concluded she had gone. He dressed and made his way down the valley a walk in which he would normally have rejoiced in the views and the play of evening sunlight on the fells, but all he saw was the girl, and all his eyes sought was to glimpse her, but the valley was empty.

Ken abandoned his plans for the rest of his stay and instead made a systematic but futile search for the girl.

Back home Ken tried to forget the pool incident and pretend it never took place. He buried himself in work, with the result that his business succeeded well, and Ken diluted his pain with a high standard of life - a big house and car - expensive holidays - you know the sort of thing.

Nothing worked, he could not erase that one glorious memory.

He tried one or two affairs but in each case it became clear to both parties that his heart was elsewhere.

Years passed and Ken just got older. Although his life had become comfortably stable - all that was about to change - the past was about to haunt him.

-

As these things sometimes do shocks can appear from nowhere, a hurricane from a clear blue sky.

Our Ken was holidaying on the south coast some distance from home and his northern industrial business. He was lunching at an innocent local pub when like a bolt of lightening crashing through his mind and burning into his heart - he saw her.

She was sitting not fifty feet away at a nearby table. his whole being knew with a searing certainty that it was she; a bit older, more mature perhaps but by her smile and her frequent laughter he knew her, by her azure eyes he knew her, by her gestures he knew her. As he sat there stunned a second more devastating shock nearly overwhelmed him - with the girl was a young lad whom he was certain he also knew well - and seconds later he knew why, he was looking at a much younger version of himself.

The pair were in the company of a confident looking man of about his own age.

As he watched with a racing heart, two important things became obvious, the man and the boy treated each other as father and son, and they were celebrating the boy's birthday - his eighteenth. With a sadness that caused him profound pain he knew that he was looking at his own son.

He wanted to pay and leave but fascination held him. The group were happy and complete. In spite of a terrible urge to go over and declare ownership of his son he knew how disturbing this would be for all four, and whatever he felt - this he could not, would not do.

With a tremendous struggle of will, and after a last long look at the happy group he left.

Ken returned to his hotel, went to his room clutching a bottle of whiskey and wept long bitter tears of regret.

We should wish our story would end there, but it does not.

In spite of doing his best to continue with his holiday plans he kept coming across the girl, the man and Ken's son. Almost by accident he learned that the girl and the man were married and that the man had adopted the boy. He also found that they lived locally.

Ken knew that for his own peace of mind he must return North to his business and put the past behind him; which to some extent he did; at least the first part - the second proved impossible.

After struggling with the memory which never left him of the girl and their son for over a year he gave in and with ultimately disastrous results to his business he moved it and himself down South, not to the same town but to an adjacent one. This did in fact give him some ease. He could now and again visit the district where he had discovered they lived, just to be near and catch an occasional glimpse. His excuse to himself was that he would be on standby if they needed him.

As it turned out he became the one in need.

The South of England is in many ways different from the North, and whereas his business flourished up North It started to fail almost immediately following the move. He got himself into legal tangles which he lost disastrously and within a few years was in considerable financial difficulties, in order to save his business he poured more money into his failing company.

In the meantime however he had followed his son's progress through university and had seen him get a well paid job with the local police force as a forensic scientist.

He had also, more recently, witnessed at a distance the girls illness and subsequent death, and had attended her funeral service albeit anonimously. Her gravestone displayed her name - Sylvia Kent, and he visited it often.

A couple of years later Ken's life had changed for the worse. His business had failed, the money he owed also took his house and all he owned. He had taken to drink and was living rough simply held together by local charity. After two more years of living like this his health began to fail - but still he drank when he could get the means.

He missed the fact that Jo Kent, his son's adopted father had also died in a car accident when on business in America.

Ken was now near his end and still the memory of that Lakeland day in the pool haunted him. It would be his last thought in this life.

***

Now at this time Johnny Kent was a very busy chap. There had been a couple of suspicious deaths which he had been able to shed light on, when they brought in the immaciated body of an elderly vagrant which had been found wrapped in old sacking in a local disused barn. Nobody claimed him or knew who he was, and Johnny was asked to use his skills to see if he could be identified.

Johnny decided that there was just a slim chance that the man's DNA profile might be on the police database.

So he took a sample.

Now Johnny's own DNA profile was already on the database for elimination purposes and to his astonishment the system found a match - the tramp with himself. In shock he ran the tests several times - with the same result. There was no doubt this shred of a human being was in fact his own biological father

Johnny tried hard but never found out any more about his real father, the only other information he had was the story told him by his mother before she died of his conception by a pool in the lakes with a lovely and loving stranger.

Johnny buried his father by the side of his mother with a headstone which read -

> 'Here lies the father of John Kent
> loved once by Sylvia Kent'

It was all he could do for the sad old tramp who was his father.

JML
5/11/2005

❦ **POWER** ❧

*Y*ou might argue that William Joseph Tangent was at the top of his game. Well educated, intelligent, and strong willed he regarded himself as a powerful man. As managing director of a successful group of companies he believed in being master of every critical business situation - Indeed Bill's rule had raised Champions, as he had named the group, to the dizzy heights of being quoted on the London Stock Exchange. Champions was Bill's whole life with one very big exception - football. These two all consuming passions took up all of his time and concentration.

He had married early more out of consideration than out of love. Katherine had left her university early to marry Bill and had spent the next several years bringing up two very capable girls now both happily married with families of there own and who now lived some distance away.

Conversation Between Bill and Katherine was strictly limited to mere domestic matters. Katherine was not interested in football nor was she involved in the high finances of Champions.

This non communication had long since invaded their marriage bed where love making had been reduced to a short, routine formality, whence both parties unbeknownst to the other were glad when it was over; that is on the few occasions it took place at all.

When Bill was free of business concerns he would sink into his, it had to be his, easy chair with pride of viewing of the huge TV set and concentrate his whole attention on football. Not all Bill's football was TV however as he always tried to make it to the ground for home games of his local team. His contributions to the club had earned him a permanent seat in the club gallery where he was well known.

But more often than not he would watch in the relative comfort of his own house.

Katherine - 'How was business today dear?'

The ball had just floated across the centre but there was no one there to take it, another chance missed.

Bill - 'Damn it where was the striker? - What? OK.'

Katherine - 'Would cottage pie be all right for dinner?'

A defender was being shown a yellow card.

Bill - 'Idiot! - What? Yes OK.'

Bill's contribution to a two way conversation was minimal if not zero. This was not helped by Katherine's inability to grasp even the basics of football or the rudiments of big business.

But this was about to change.

One bright golden evening, with Bill engrossed in a cup- tie, Katherine, after the usual pleasantries answered by Bill's grunts, said,

'I'm considering starting an Open University course possibly something to do with finance.'

The goalie had fumbled the ball on the goal line and the ref was consulting the linesmen.

'Great - What the hell, it was in. Is he blind? Get him a damn blind dog.' Replied Bill.

And that was that, and she did.

After much hard work which to her surprise she thoroughly took to and enjoyed, Katherine succeeded, and attained a good degree in business studies. Her choice of subject was such that she might be able at last to have a proper conversation with her husband.

'I've just got my results dear.'

The opposition were in the defender's half and in possession.

'For heavens sake someone tackle that man - What?'

'My OU results have come and I've got my degree.'

Now the opposing team had forced a corner. The ball had soared over a bunch of coloured shirts in the goal mouth and after a scramble was cleared well up-field.

'Christ, that was close - What? Oh great, well done. Defence was half asleep, a mess if ever I saw one.'

Katherine spent some time deciding to what use to put her new found knowledge. An unexpected secondary effect of her success was a tremendous boost to her self confidence. After careful consideration she decided to apply for a job with a small local business firm. This she did and was immediately accepted. Her university training was just what they needed and they liked her.

'I hope you won't mind dear I have just accepted a job with Hardys on the industrial estate. I should be home in time to prepare dinner most days and when not there will always be something to microwave.'

This was a long speech for Katherine, and she was expecting one of Bill's disinterested comments, but it was half time and the usual 'experts' were uninteresting.

'Crikey! What's the world coming to? You with a job eh!'

Bill was confident that it wouldn't last, and the second half whistle had just been sounded.

Now Katherine's job not only lasted but proved a great success for both her and Hardys. Over a couple of years the company grew and with it came Katherine's promotion through the ranks of the management team and to her satisfaction and surprise she found herself at the head of the company. A company about to expand. All this Katherine conveyed to Bill as usual mixed in with a TV commentary. But Bill's mind was disengaged from the serious import of what Katherine was telling him.

He therefore did not see what misfortune was about to befall him.

It was during this period that Bill's company, Champions, hit a shaky patch with heavy competition and no new products, and Bill was having to spend less time at home and on his precious football. He gave even less attention to what his wife had to say.

Sadly this extra load on Bill meant that their sporadic love making drifted into total stagnation.

It was now that it happened, unexpected and shattering.

Tired and unhappy Bill sank into 'his' chair with a large whiskey, switched on the set and settled down to be cheered up by a hour's scheduled soccer.

Oh dear.

The man on TV was very apologetic but due to exceptionally bad weather at the away ground the football match had been postponed. It would be replaced by highlights of previous games. As this was of no interest to Bill he switched over to the news.

It was nearly the last item of news that caused Bill to sit up in his chair and spill his whiskey down his shirt front.

There had been a stock-market raid with the result that Hardys now owned Champions. Not only that but there was the TV news hound interviewing the head of Hardys - none other than his own wife.

Bill thought he was dreaming - Katherine, his own wife.

With a pounding heart he tried to make out what she had to say. This was the very first time that Bill had really listened to her.

'It's not so much a takeover,' she was saying, 'It's more of a merger. The companies complement each other, and their combination presents an excellent business opportunity.'

In reply to the question on redundancies she said there may be some slimming down, but it would probably be in management and not the workforce which may need to be expanded to meet the challenge of the future.

And that was it. Bill simply sat there stunned, whiskey and football forgotten. Eventually anger and fear possessed his being in equal measure, he was now in a totally unfamiliar world. He could only await Katherine's return, his mind at a loss to know what to expect, the man of power was now dispossessed of its supporting strength.

Now, in fairness to Bill; Katherine had not been listening either. When Bill had mentioned Champions she had assumed that he was referring to his football team and not the company. The very first time she came to associate the firm with Bill was that evening after the TV interview when just before she left the office she picked up a piece of paper on which were listed the Board of Directors of Champions. And she was shaken to her very core when she saw Bill's name at the very top.

Worse - she had decided to interview each of Champion's directors to decide their future, if any, with the company, and the letters requesting their presence had gone out; Bill would get his on Monday for an interview on Tuesday which meant that they had the intervening weekend to face.

She sat there stunned, cup of coffee forgotten. Disapointment and fear gripped her in equal measure. Reluctant now to set off for home, nevertheless she knew the problem and Bill had to be faced.

On arriving home she found Bill as we had left him stiff and upright in his chair looking at a blank TV set, his back a wall of anger and resentment.

Several times over the next two days Katherine tried to explain but Bill was unreachable. They had reached a point where they were gripped in a power struggle which had to be resolved.

On Monday Bill got his letter and face red with pent-up fury said through clenched teeth,

'I will be there, I wouldn't miss it for anything.'

Things were black indeed and Katherine felt that this was the end of their marriage. Bill wished everyone to hell.

***

Tuesday, and the fates were set to do their worst.

Bill duly arrived and got someone to park his company Bentley and was promptly shown up to Katherine's office.

He was immediately impressed by the air of quiet efficiency about the place.

'Good morning Sir, Mrs Tangent is expecting you. Please go right in, would you like coffee?'

Bill said yes to coffee and went in.

Now Bill had realised that this was make or break time for him, and though he knew he had no high cards to play he was determined to gain control of the situation and the company. After all he had been in the business a long time and knew all the wrinkles. He had fought management battles before and was used to winning. With only his wife as opposition he felt confident, and betrayed, and anger rose in him.

However, on entering he was completely taken aback by the sheer size and opulence of the office and the amount and range of the electronic equipment on the vast desk behind which his wife sat.

She did not get up.

'Hallo Bill, please sit down.' She said indicating one of the easy chairs opposite her.

Bill stood.

'What the hell is this all about? You will not get away with it - I still control Champions.' He ground out.

'Do please sit down.' Katherine replied ominously quietly.

'I'm not here to stay - I am here to tell you what's what and to get back to my business.' And he spun round to lean over the big desk.

There was a long pause, then -

'I said sit down, so sit down.' Katherine was trembling, she had never in all their married life dared to speak to Bill like this.

And to her surprise, and his, Bill sat.

At this point following a light knock on the door the secretary came in pushing a trolley with coffee and biscuits, and quietly left.

Katherine dealt coffee for them both during the neutral silence which followed. This then was it, she thought. It must be now.

'This is how it will be,' she said gathering all her strength. 'I have here a list of tasks for you which I expect you to accomplish in one week. You will therefore report here at 9 am next Tuesday to report on these actions - and I expect them to be completed.'

Bill was aghast. He took the list with a shaking hand and glanced down it and knew it was a tough challenge.

'And what if I don't?' He spat out.

Katherine sat back and looked at Bill for a long time and knew the thrill of power.

'Then you will loose your job.' She said quietly.

Bill slowly rose and without another word headed for the door. At the door he turned to face his wife, but could not find any words. So he just left.

Disaster? We shall see.

Bill's first reaction was to tear up the action list and pen his resignation. His second and completely unexpected reaction was one of excitement. He had never seen his wife like this and it attracted him enormously. As he felt the power she now held over him he found a deep rooted desire to succumb to her will. He was falling in love with this strange masterful person.

Katherine on the other hand had never before drunk the extraordinary heady wine of power and was shaken to find it very palatable. She felt that she wanted to drink more of this intoxicating stuff and was looking forward to bringing some of it home. And she did.

She was home first and the first thing Bill noticed on arrival was that the TV had been turned ever so slightly so that it now faced both easy chairs equally.

This powershift now invaded their bedroom where their lovemaking was long and satisfying with Bill happily responding to his wife's demands.

And afterwards Katherine said - 'And you will take me to the next football match and get someone to explain the rules to me.'

Bill snuggled down and smiled at the darkness. Whilst Katherine, just before she drifted into sleep, wondered vaguely who had won, and then realised that it mattered not at all.

And life was just great.

JML
14/11/2005

⟨ **THE SUPER RUNNER** ⟩

$\mathcal{I}$t was in the summer of 2086 and it is still talked about to this day ten years on.

Technology and in particular bio-technology had advanced considerably since the early 2000'nds. The principal changes were the establishment of a world government and thus world political control and the compulsory brain embedded chip. This device invisible externally was connected to all of the main control centers in the brain and was fitted at birth to every one of earth's citizens.

The implications of this process were far reaching. It meant that most anti-social tendencies could be modified by changing the stored control data in an individual's chip. And this by means of a painless procedure applied without surgery by electronic coupling to an external computer.

Thus 'patients' suffering from alcoholism, drug addiction, aggression, or depression, for example, could have their condition ameliorated by a simple visit to their GP.

This advance produced for the first time world peace that is until much later when hackers had found their own way to modify the chips, and the whole system was hurriedly abandoned.

Harry C'Obeen was never sure if his parents, long since expired, had named him Harry as a joke or for some other unknown reason that died with them. Nicknamed Beany by his colleagues and much worse by his schoolmates, Harry was a normal young man happy under control of his brain chip. Unfortunately he fell in love with and married Harriet also known to her friends as Harry.

What Harry did not expect was that the C'Obeens would become world famous, and could never have dreamed how.

Now one of the effects of this system of human control was the general levelling off of peaks of excitement, the ups and downs of emotion were smoothed out. This in turn meant that life became quite humdrum even boring.

Harriet was constantly if dully aware that something was missing from their love making, over and done with in a matter of moments it left her with a nearly overwhelming sense of longing. Harry too was aware of something lacking.

Indeed the overall effect of the brain chip was to create in the individual a deep running current of frustration which found its outlet in the intense and over the top pursuit of so called hobbies and pastimes.

For instance Harry became involved in home improvement, whilst Harriet took up cooking. We are not talking here of mere amateur activities, these two good people were engaged in wholesale and complete dedication to their chosen areas of activity.

Harriet would come home from a couple of day's with a friend only to find in parking her car that the garage had gone and been replaced by a library. Harry on the other hand might be faced with a thirty-two course banquet and be expected to try and comment on each dish.

Once Harriet made some very special little cakes which she placed in the oven to cook. returning later to see how they were doing she not only found they were not there but neither was the cooker. Harry was busy modifying the kitchen layout.

It was not uncommon for Harriet to arrive home and let herself in via her front door and for a moment think she was in the wrong house because the whole layout had been changed, and entering the lounge would find herself in a small wardrobe or downstairs toilet newly built by Harry.

On another occasion opening a door she had only just perceived she nearly fell down a flight of stairs into the bowels of a cellar that she was sure was not there before. Weekly the wall decorations or the curtains were changed and the furniture rearranged almost daily so that sitting down to watch a bit of tele she would find herself looking at a floor to ceiling bookcase full of encyclopedias or a window looking out into a new greenhouse full of healthy looking tomato plants. Once on going to bed late one night she had wakened at dawn to find herself fully exposed on a balcony overlooking the road.

Harry just never stopped.

He on the other hand was faced with daily experimental cooking. In the whole of their married life he had never ever had the same dish twice. To say to Harriet he enjoyed some exotic preparation was a sure way to ensure he would never see the likes of it ever again. A seventeen course meal was routine to Harriet, and Harry was expected to sample it all.

And yet the chip ensured mutual tolerance.

For a time.

It was the weather that changed everything.

On a hot and sultry day in early spring, Harry was out of doors digging the foundations for a new extension he had planned. Storm clouds were brewing and he was anxious to cover the trench before the threatened rain began. As the first large drops darkened the ground the scene was shakily lit by a searing flash of lightening which was almost immediately followed by a ear splitting tearing sound and then a very loud series of bangs. Harry was thrown to the ground where he lay for some time dazed and partially deaf.

On picking himself up he found that apart from being somewhat shaken he felt quite normal and continued to finish off the work he had planned for the day.

However a tiny part of him had been subtley modified.

After dinner of some nine courses Harry and Harriet retired to the lounge and sat in front of their in house entertainment system. Harriet picked up the universal electronic controller and switched on the system. For a time all was well but then Harry asked his wife to 'fast forward' to a more interesting part of the program.

It was then that a strange thing happened.

Harry not only started to speak extremely quickly but his movements became so fast they were just a blur.

'Whatthehell'sgoing on?' He said.

'I'm sure I don't know dear I just pressed fast forward on the controller.' Harriet replied.

To illustrate this she pressed replay and to both of their astonishment Harry became very slow.

'N o w   w h a t ' s   h a p p e n i n g ?' Harry ground out.

'It's this thing it seems to be affecting you.' She said in a puzzled tone. And so saying she pressed 'pause' and Harry just stopped moving, he simply sat there like a statue.

On pressing 'play' Harry returned to normal.

Further experiments revealed that only these three functions affected Harry. And to his intense annoyance Harriet insisted in making Harry go slow fast and stop in turn and refused to give up the controller. Later she agreed only to use it with his consent.

However that night in bed and able to control the speed at which Harry did things Harriet created a love making marathon and for the first time they both achieved a level of contented satisfaction.

For some time after this the three 'Harry' controller buttons were only used for love making.

But one fateful day the 'fast forward' button was pressed when Harry was out running and he quickly reached a speed where he was easily overtaking all the traffic, - he was just a blur.

Our good couple then put there heads together and decided 'just for fun' to enter Harry as a runner in the local amateur sports day. And this they did.

On the day Harry, the unknown quantity, was regarded with some curiosity by the other competitors who agreed that he did not look fit enough to provide a serious challenge.

They had entered Harry in the all comers 500 meters.

Soon the competitors were lined up for the start. 'Set.' Shouted the starter and gun fired and Harriet in her excitement pressed the wrong button and Harry started OK but in slow mode. The rest of the field streaked ahead leaving an increasing gap between themselves and Harry. Then

Harriet found the right button and a gasp of astonishment rose from the crowd as Harry simply hurtled past the rest, finishing a good 100 meters ahead of the field.

A ragged shout went up from the crowd, runners and spectators gathered around Harry who was nearly overwhelmed by all the questions fired at him.

He collected his small trophy presented by some local dignitary and he and Harriet sneaked away to avoid any more difficult queries especially from the local press.

Now they knew they had cheated but it had been fun and Harry had enjoyed being the centre of attention.

So they agreed to do one more amateur race meeting and this time they would run 'fast forward' from the start.

The day came and soon the runners were away to the starting gun. Harry nearly vanished in a mist of arms and legs. The man with the stop watch nearly dropped it when its speed reading notched 50 miles per hour.

This time the press would not let Harry go - they hardly believed what they had seen. Eventually knowledge of Harry's amazing performance reached the national press.

Over the following weeks Harry, now a national hero, was persuaded to do a demonstration run with a professional timekeeping system to record his performance.

***

The trial took place in one of the largest of our football stadiums, and to Harry's dismay a huge crowd had turned up.

But so had the nations press and TV.

A nervous Harriet and an even more nervous Harry made themselves ready, and to a hushed crowd Harry readied himself at the start.

BANG. Harriet pressed 'fast forward' and Harry hurtled forward at a terrific pace.

But he had not gone far when he suddenly slowed to walking speed, then equally suddenly speeded off again only to jerk to a complete halt moments later.

It mattered not what Harriet did with her controller nothing she did made any difference to Harry's continuing fast, slow, stop, slow, stop, fast, and so on round the course.

The commentators and TV controllers were operating their own command units and unknowingly directly affecting Harry's progress.

The crowed found their voice, feeling they had been cheated, roared their disapproval, and piled out of the stadium loudly demanding a full refund for their tickets.

Harry ran for it, fortunately he was on 'fast forward' and managed to escape with Harriet.

They knew they couldn't go home where the press would be in waiting, so they found a quiet hotel and booked in for a week.

During that week the on-going press furore made them decide to leave the country anonymously and set up home again in some distant part of the world where no one needed or owned Universal electronic controllers. They kept theirs of course to use only for love making.

Harry having disabled the pause button - just in case.

JML
2/12/05

❦ A HOLIDAY TREAT ❧

He was alone, on holiday, away from home and very bored.

The pub was pleasant enough and the food was excellent but he had eaten there for the last three evenings and was beginning to wish that he had tried somewhere else.

Whilst sitting with the menu at the bar he decided to keep his mind active by studying the other guests.

There in the corner were the usual non-speaking tired looking middle aged couple gazing at the world with dead eyes in dead faces - there is always one he thought. He felt for a moment like going over and shaking them up but reflected that this was probably not possible.

A family group attracted his attention. Lively with two youngsters they laughed and joked seemingly all the time, and tonight he found himself envying them.

He sipped his pint of Bass, and lost interest in his survey.

Then, scanning the quickly filling bar, his eyes lit on a girl who appeared to be on her own. She wandered, a little apprehensively, he thought, into the light of the bar and with an elegant swish of her skirt swung herself onto an adjacent stool. She had obviously been here before because the barman said a pleasant Good Evening and would she like her usual?

'Please,' she said.

Seemingly self contained she took no interest in the other customers, simply sitting quietly with her drink.

As he tried not to stare at the newcomer, nevertheless he slowly became aware that there was something familiar about this girl. Something in the past? Something; an incident, emotionally highly charged? He couldn't be sure it was she, it was a long time ago. If it was the same one would she recognise him? Would she remember?

As he tried to solve the mystery she turned and gave him a quick smile, and he was almost sure, his heart acknowledged it.

God! she's certainly attractive he thought. Long tawny hair, green eyes in an intelligent face, and a figure to match - both elegant and curvacious. Neatly dressed any man would be proud to be with her. His heart tumbled and she noticed his stare.

He had to say something but felt tongue tied.

'Good evening.' Was all he could manage.

'Hallo,' she replied.

Then came the words he would remember for ever.

'Could I possibly borrow your menu?'

'Sure. Help yourself,' he responded.

Then, hesitantly -

'It doesn't matter what you choose, it's all good here.'

She sat silently with a delightful frown and contemplated the choices. This allowed him to study her directly, and as he did he struggled for a name - he was still not sure that it was she - time would have changed her.

But as he looked the vague memories were replaced by a strong natural desire.

Suddenly she looked up directly at him and their eyes met. Her smile turned his heart over and he stared at her with open admiration.

Their gaze of mutual appraisal was interrupted by the barman asking if they had decided what to order.

'Yes,' he managed, and ordered what he had had previously.

The girl placed her order and the barman said he would tell them when it would be ready.

He had difficulty believing that such a lovely girl would be eating alone. But had they met before? Something about her still resonated in his mind.

'Are you here on holiday?' He ventured.

'No,' she replied. 'I'm here visiting my elderly auntie.'

'Is she unwell?' He asked, genuinely concerned.

'Not she,' she replied. 'Even at eighty two she has more energy than me. She is studying an Open University course in literature, and doing exceptionally well.'

At this she paused as if unsure whether or not to continue to tell him more, and then -.

'I'm here for the rest of the week and thoroughly enjoying the change of scenery, I probably won't want to return,' then added 'and you?'

'On holiday, also till the end of the week,' he told her.

They then started an animated discussion about the place and the locals, the scenery, and the weather - which had been cheerfully sunny.

It was at a natural pause in their discourse that a waiter appeared and advised them that the table was ready.

The table!

It had clearly been assumed by the staff that they were together.

He thought she would object to this arrangement and took the waiter's arm to explain the mistake, but to his astonishment and glee she stopped him.

Now what was happening? Had she recognised him? The thought filled him with anticipation and made him fearful at the same time.

The food arrived and they both found their conversation interesting and amusing. They might have been friends for years.

They found that they were both divorced, but her name when she told him meant nothing and she made no response to his.

He must know, he thought, and taking a deep breath -.

'Did you go to university?' He asked.

She was silent for some time.

'Yes, Manchester,' she admitted eventually.

At this he said nothing for a while, thinking.

He took a chance.

'I've had a feeling that we must have met somewhere before, I couldn't be sure, it seems so long ago, almost another world, but I took a science degree at Manchester.'

He stated the time he was there, and to his delight she said that was when she was there also.

At this they both concentrated on the food and were silent, each was considering the implications of this latest attestation.

Then followed a cautious and hesitant exchange of university memories.

There was a subtle change of mood. The very air was, it seemed, tingling with electricity.

It was as if they were both fencing.

Then came the moment.

He knew he had fallen for her, he was under her spell.

Throwing caution to the winds he plunged ahead.

'Do you remember Bill's twenty-first? I'm sure you were there?'

He had said it at last.

The girl sat for a long time with a grave expression, and a look of recognition slowly dawning on her very pretty face.

She hesitated, then -

'Er............yes?'

It was a question.

'We had a lot to drink.' He included her.

'I remember walking you to your digs.' This time it was just her.

At this she broke the spell by stating that she would like another drink.

They talked inconsequentially. He described the self catering accommodation he had hired, and she waxed lyrical about the place her aunt owned.

Well that's that, he thought, the end of a sweet but very short friendship.

He was just about to wind things up when -.

'I do remember that party and someone taking me home,' she admitted.

He plunged ahead -.

'It must have been me.' He stopped. Then in a hurry -.

'And I stayed the night.'

There. It had been said, and he waited for her reaction.

Then very softly, her green eyes on his.

'Yes,' she said, 'I remember, and it was lovely.'

He found he was sweating with the strain of not offending her and thus loosing everything.

Nothing was said for a long long time. But conversation did get going again, and now there was an understanding between them.

She phoned her aunt, and he took her to his accommodation where they spent the night delighting each other in expressions of physical love.

***

The following morning he made breakfast, and conversation was merry and intimate.

Arms on the table, hands clutching a cup of coffee, she silently surveyed him with those beautiful knowing green eyes.

'I have a confession to make,' she said.

His heart stopped. He had no inkling of what was to come, and when it did it was a shock.

He waited tense with dread.

'I never was at Manchester University. In fact I have never been to Manchester,' she added in a whisper.

He looked astonished, but she said no more.

Silence filled the room and strong emotions swirled about.

He heaved a great sigh.

'I also have a confession,' he said.

'Neither was I.

JML
20/12/2005

A QUIET WOMAN

At the age of fifty Brendon Cordon was a reasonably contented man. He held down a reasonably remunerative job, he had raised two reasonably successful sons, now married and away, and was enjoying the fruits of a life of reasonably hard work.

At twenty five he had fallen for and married Maureen Booth. What had attracted him to her was that she was a quiet person, quiet that is in almost every respect. She was very self contained, taking the rough with the smooth with equal equanimity. Amazingly she handled her children without the need ever to raise her voice to scold them, and was equally adept with other peoples off-spring. In discussions she would make her points patiently but with a firmness that had to be accounted.

An attractive woman, she had a sensitive and loving nature which Brendon enjoyed and encouraged especially in the privacy of their bedroom.

Brendon himself was not given to high excitement having a somewhat placid nature himself. The only time he had been known to raise his voice was in support of his local football team Sheffield United.

Their life together was a model of tranquillity, it was in fact humdrum - even boring.

This marital peace was however not destined to last.

Under Maureen's placid exterior another more volatile individual was invisably growing.

Now Brendon had a brother a couple of years younger than himself.

James shared Brendon's liking for a peaceful life. He also had a well paid and stable job and living as they did close to each other they often met, and enjoying similar pastimes got on well,

Superficially their only serious difference was that James was an avid supporter of Sheffield Wednesday, but even this was taken at a humerous level.

James however was a much more determined individual. Under his jokes and pleasantries lay a hard and selfdetermined mind. He knew what he wanted and got it, much in contrast to Brendon's accommodating nature.

Now Brendon's brother James had met and married Alice, Maureen's sister who was just two years her junior. They also had brought up two children, now married, in their case daughters; but here any similarity between the two sisters ended.

Alice was as noisy and volatile as Maureen was quiet. She was a very lovely girl but she just never stopped talking, that is - never.

She talked from dawn till dusk, and even in her sleep. She talked through breakfast, lunch and dinner, she talked whilst reading, during music concerts and television. If she couldn't find anyone to talk to she would be on the phone. And what a boon her mobile was to her.

She was not unintelligent, nor poorly educated, much of her conversation was to the point and often witty - it just never seemed to stop.

'It says in the paper the Prime Minister can't last much longer, he should never have married that wife of his, why he goes abroad so much one can just imagine, and never taking her with him. And all that heat in what's it called? And always wearing a suit, no wonder he always looks so bedraggled. What with ....' And so on and on.

'Are you going to the match this Saturday? Don't forget your tickets, it says it might rain you had better take an umbrella, is Brendon going?...............'

'Yes dear.' Umbrella indeed - at a soccer match!

Now when James and Alice were first married, Alice's bubbly spontaneous nature was the great attraction for James. It was new to him, and seemed fresh and exciting and won them many good friends. As the children were growing up they absorbed much of Alice's volubility, allowing James to be selective in what he listened to.

But since now there was only the two of them every word was directed at him.

And he could not find the off button.

It began as a mild irritation and grew into a strong irritation and sometimes a fury which he only just succeeded in bottling up, after all a peaceful life was all he asked for.

But he found that more and more he was making excuses to go round to Brendon's where he could bask in their wonderful healing peace.

And it adversely affected their love life which he could now only enjoy if he had a certain amount to drink, and would be over quickly so that he didn't have to listen to

Alice's running commentary on all and everything. He took to sleeping apart.

A storm was brewing.

Tensions in both houses were reaching breaking point when fate stepped in, unnoticed at the time. It took the shape of Brendon's work requiring him to spend several months in the far east.

He and Maureen agreed that as she reacted badly to heat it would be best if he went alone.

This was not a good idea but they had little choice as Brendon's pension depended on his keeping his job.

Fate had played its card.

Brendon duly set off, and was soon only a voice on the phone albeit nearly every day.

James and Brendon had agreed, as brothers should, that whilst Brendon was away James would keep an eye on Maureen and help her out when required.

And James obliged - in spades.

He now had a heaven made excuse to avoid the ever noisy Alice and enjoy the company of the ever quiet Maureen. Occasional visits to check if averything was OK were soon more frequent and longer visits and then even longer visits.

James had realised what he wanted and set out to get it. If his conscience troubled him he didn't show it. He decided that he would have his way in total disregard of the feelings of Brendon, Alice or anyone else who got in his way.

And what he would have was Maureen - and peace at last.

So his visits to his brother's house became the means of seduction.

At first Maureen did not understand what James's intentions were, and confided her longings for a slightly more exciting life to him. She trusted him and allowed him familiarities hitherto reserved for her husband, and soon she began to miss him when he returned to Alice.

James took full advantage of her every weakness and eventually on the feeble excuse of a possible break-in stayed the night.

Alice now knew the score, she too had trusted James, and was shocked and surprised by what had happened. She wept bitter tears of pain and anguish. But she knew her James and that he would not now be diverted. She wrote a long sad letter to Brendon who was coming to the end of his term abroad and who now made plans to return and deal with his traitor of a brother.

Brendon returned but to Alice's and his distress appeals to James and to Maureen had no effect.

James took the quiet Maureen away and after explaining matters to all four children set up house with her and put his own house up for sale. He did however agree to half the proceeds going to his wife.

At the time James's house was being handed over Alice had nowhere to go. Both daughters had houses full and she was reluctant to impose herself on them.

She had become used to discussing their mutual tragedy with Brendon. And so he suggested as a temporary measure only, and until she found a place of her own, he would put her up.

At first this arrangement worked well, but soon Alice's constant chatter started to cause Brendon to avoid her company as much as possible.

But then a strange thing happened.

Alice was of an age when women approach the change of life. A change in the balance of female hormones sometimes results it significant changes in emotions and occasionally in behaviour.

At first Brendon noticed nothing because the change was so very gradual. But one day he could not help but become aware that Alice had spent the whole evening watching TV with him and had hardly said a word. He thought she might be unwell but his concerned enquiries resulted her assurance that she was never better and perfectly happy.

Brendon soon found that this change was not a one off, but was on the increase - Alice was in fact becoming a quiet woman.

This new Alice was a delight to Brendon who began to enjoy her company as much as before he had sought to avoid it. They went on holiday together, which was a great success, and on their return by mutual consent they agreed to share the same bed. Their four children visited often and were amazed and pleased by their parents obvious love for each other.

***

Meanwhile, James and Maureen had toured the world, and returned to enjoy the rest of their lives together.

But here fate proved unkind.

Being of a similar age to her sister Maureen was also undergoing the change of life, but in her case things did not go well. She had some pain and spent some time away with one of her daughters to recover.

It was on her return that James immediately noticed the difference. Gone was the quiet person he ran away with, here was a woman who could not and would not stop talking.

At his insistence they moved into separate bedrooms.

He looked forward to his coming retirement with considerable dread, and their children were fearful for their future which promised to be a most unhappy and noisesome one. They had begun to profoundly dislike one another.

JML
30/12/2005

⊰ **TOO GOOD TO BE TRUE** ⊱

He just could not take his eyes off her. She was filling his mind. Everything else around almost ceased to exist. He was mightily glad that he was not with another girl who would certainly object to his wayward attention. A work colleague and good friend had brought and introduced him to the party hosts but had then left him to pursue his own objective.

The girl was as vivacious as she was gloriously handsome. She seemed to know everyone or rather everyone knew her. The very centre of attention wherever she was, she appeared completely at ease.

Sparkling intelligent brown-green eyes set in a french face appraised her listener with her complete attention whenever she was addressed.

Her figure whilst slender was still determindly feminine, her whole being lithe with vitality, her evening gown a mere caress.

He had never seen anyone like her and he was smitten, hooked, even without meeting her he was her slave.

Since he had eyes for no one else it was only a matter of time before she noticed his worshipping stares; and to his surprise she made her way across the room to stand there facing him. For him at that moment there was only the two of them in the whole world.

But as is often the case he did not know what on earth to say. Then -

'My name is Vicky, but you must call me Vee.'

Her voice churned his inside, soft and melodic it matched the rest of her and the spell was unbroken.

'I'm George, and I am very pleased to meet you.' He managed after a pause to get his breath.

'Have you been here before?' She asked.

'No,' he replied, 'I was introduced by a friend.'

'Are you enjoying it?'

'I am now that I have met you.'

He knew this sounded gauche but it was out before he could stop himself; and anyway he really meant it.

She gave one of her low chuckles that he was to come to know so well.

'Come on then, bring your drink and let's wander onto the balcony where we can have a good chat.'

He could not believe his luck, and simply followed her totally captivated as he was.

He recovered some composure and they really did talk. He told her about himself making sure that she understood that even at the ripe old age of 24 he was still un-attached.

She it appeared came from a good county set bred family had independent means and was also un-attached.

Drinks finished, conversation at a pause, he was wondering what next when suddenly and amazingly, on a whim she grabbed his hand and ran with him out to where the cars were parked. Here she held open the passenger door of a big and very expensive sports car. He climbed in, his mind a jumble of excitement.

She drove, as he was to find she did most things, easily and well.

With the immediate future now in the girl's hands he relaxed as she headed towards the setting sun; gliding effortlessly along quiet lanes.

Eventually she parked in a lonely spot overlooking the sea. The sun was just a blood red arc on the horizon staining the water with its dying light. One or two stars were beginning to show. And here, for the first time she kissed him.

Their affair was a whirl of meetings, parties, trips and long, long nights.

They made love in her very large and opulent flat on her massive sumptuous bed.

And he was hers.

But she remained a puzzle to him. She would not take him to meet her folks and was disinclined to meet his. She refused to discuss their future, and disconcertingly when together she would vanish for some time and avoided all attempts on his part to discover where she had been. In these instances she would return breathless and with eyes that hid secrets.

She was accepted at most of the large local estates, and would take him with her to garden parties and dances of which there always seemed to be one at any given time.

He observed that she was wealthy and merely assumed that this came from her family.

After some months these gaps in their relationship started to tell. The girl got annoyed by his probing questions, and he became more concerned at her prevarications and excuses.

One day he tried to follow her but she drove so fast that he had enormous difficulty keeping her speeding car in sight, and soon she was lost in the town traffic. He became convinced the she knew she was being chased and had deliberately set out to loose him. When challenged she simply denied all knowledge of the incident.

But he was still besotted with her and although unhappy with the situation always inevitably gave in.

Then fate took a hand and George found out the hard way, and the effect nearly killed him.

They were due to meet at a dance at a local landowner's place in celebration of his daughter's coming of age.

The time of their meeting was set for nine p.m., but George got the time wrong thinking they had agreed eight p.m.; and he was late.

It had been raining hard, it was still drizzling and there was much standing water on the lanes. On a bend close to where a narrow lane joined on the left, George lost control of his car. The vehicle mounted the grass verge and slid unceremoniously and solidly into the water filled ditch.

Fortunately George was shaken but unhurt and after pulling himself together called up the RAC rescue on his mobile phone - was told they would be with him in about forty-five minutes. He used this time to phone the party host and explain what had happened and learned that the girl had as yet not arrived but that when she did they would pass on his message.

He then tried to phone her and was told by the anonymous voice that her phone was turned off - nothing therefore to do but wait for the RAC man. He turned on the radio, found a suitable station and settled back in his seat.

In due course the RAC arrived and after weighing up the situation the man started the process of attaching a tow-rope to George's car. At this point George got out to lighten the car and wandered round the back of the car to watch proceedings. Having fixed the tow-rope the RAC man went to the front of the car to make sure all was clear.

It was now that it all happened, swiftly and seemingly without pause.

There was the growing sound of a car travelling very fast along the side road. It arrived at the junction close by where the RAC man was standing and turned up the road ahead almost losing control. It was travelling very fast and was soon out of sight. George at the back did not see much of this and ran round to see if the RAC man was OK. He found him still standing looking after the disappearing car and muttering quiet oaths under his breath.

They discussed what had happened with mutual disapprobation, and had just set about their task again when the peace was torn apart by the strident shriek of police sirens. No less than three police cars came speeding down the lane, two went up the side road whilst the third pulled up beside them, and two burly policemen got out.

After ensuring George and the RAC man were OK, they proceeded to question them closely about the car they had just seen. George couldn't help much having been unsighted but the RAC man gave them chapter and verse including writing the cars number in the policeman's notebook. However they were told nothing about what was going on, but were asked to report to the local police station the next day to make written statements 'for the record'.

George and his car did not get home until after midnight and he had still failed to make contact with the girl.

***

George went early to the police station the following day worried that he had still not heard from Vee.

The RAC man was already there.

Having made their statements and signed them, they were told that there had been a house break-in. The thief had been disturbed by the owner's wife who was now dead of head injuries.

All George's concern was elsewhere, and he was only half listening when he heard the RAC man say -

'And it was lucky that I got the car's registration number, it was one of those personalised ones, it was -',

He paused for effect,

'- VEE 1.'

Then George knew.

A very hurt and desperately unhappy George waited to see them bring her in.

In spite of the handcuffs she walked in still gloriously defiant, and very, very beautiful.

George had to turn away so that they would not see his tears. He knew then that whatever the future held for him, he would never love like that again.

JML
31/12/2005

⊱ GOD'S MYSTERIOUS PLAN ⊰

*J*ennifer McDivert could not fathom what was wrong. It was troubling her and seemed to be getting worse. She had inherited a strong Christian faith from her loving parents so she was not inclined to blame the All-mighty.

Her twenty-sixth birthday was rapidly approaching and she was without a regular boy friend.

She knew she was attractive to the opposite sex by the turning of men's heads and the way they regarded her. And she was not short of dates being regularly chatted up and asked out.

She had in fact had several serious relationships but for some mysterious reason they had each time come to nothing and each break up when it came caused her much anguish and self searching.

The first, apart from early teenage fumbles, was young Johnny. He had fallen for her in a big way and they became lovers. But Johnny just out of college would not have the means to support a family for some years and so their leaving home and settling down together would have to wait. It was during this period of being together and yet not being that Johnny gradually started to loose interest and found excuses ever more frequently to avoid making love. Eventually they simply drifted apart.

Jennifer was saddened and refused all comers after this for some time - but then came big Sam. He was big and brash, stood no nonsense and swept her off her feet. This relationship lasted about a year and ended as quickly as it had started when she found out that he was spending every Tuesday night with someone else. Although hurt she felt she had had a narrow escape.

But it took the gentle and sensitive Robin to cause Jennifer serious pain. The wound he delivered she knew she would carry like a scar for the rest of her life.

Robin came into her life almost unnoticed. He took a job with the same agency as Jennifer and was absorbed into the office environment without a ripple in its daily routine.

A naturally quiet person Robin went about his work disturbing no-one, fitting smoothly into the routine of the place. He had a natural gift for being ignored, but seemed always to be there when needed. He was never angry and had never been known to raise his voice in annoyance or stress.

They would never have noticed each other had the firm not thrown them together. Their mutual boss assigned them to the same two-person project.

Even then Jennifer did not anticipate what Robin would come to mean to her.

The work threw them together and very gradually Robin, by dint of his quiet steady way, made himself indispensable to the project's success. And to be fair he always acknowledged Jennifer's contribution.

At first she took his interest in her as simply keenness for the project to succeed. It was hard work which soon demanded they met for serious discussions outside the work environment and normal hours. Initially this was at a local hostelry but eventually she took him home where they could use her computer in relative peace.

From the start her parents took to Robin, his natural courtesy and quiet ways won him their affection and before very long they treated him and Jennifer as a couple, in spite of her regular protests to the contrary.

Such was the insidious nature of this regime that Jennifer herself began to think of their meetings as something more than work.

Open and forthcoming about all other topics Robin was unusually reticent about himself. Jennifer knew nothing of his background, he never mentioned his home life and seemed to have no other friends or acquaintances; a serious omission which Jennifer was soon to make the mistake of ignoring.

It was not long into the project that she began to be aware that Robin's attention was directed more to her than to the work, and found that she liked it. He appeared always to be clean and well turned out and to her eyes was not unattractive.

Then came the inevitable time when her parents took a well earned trip abroad.

She and Robin took full advantage of the empty house, and before her parents return Jennifer had decided that Robin and herself were compatible in bed as well as out of it. And in her mind she began to entertain more serious plans for them both and in this Robin did nothing to disabuse her. He allowed her to make plans for them to set up home together and even eventually to marry. The momentum of this myth carried Robin along with it, he lacked the strength of character to stop it. Afraid of hurting Jennifer he allowed her to build hopes that in their failure were to cause her even more pain.

Jennifer was completely disbelieving when the shock came.

The project came to an end, and it fell to her boss to deliver the fateful blow, unaware of the bombshell he was unleashing.

'Thank you for the excellent job you and Robin did, you clearly worked well together. It's a pity it can't continue but Robin has had to leave the firm at short notice. His fiance has had to go down south to look after her seriously ill mother and they have decided to move to be close.'

Fiance.

Jennifer was stunned.

On making enquiries she discovered that Robin had only recently got engaged - he just hadn't had the courtesy to tell her.

She asked for leave, which was granted, and went home to nurse her damaged ego and broken heart.

Most of her time was spent worrying about what was wrong and she concluded that she had so far just picked the wrong men.

It would be some time before she would look favourably at a man, but the human spirit is resilient and with the sympathetic help of her colleagues she eventually took it as a lesson learnt.

Jennifer promised herself that next time she would make sure that her man was right for her, and had no romantic attachments.

She was given a new recruit to train, a charming girl of a similar age to herself, the new girl introduced her to a friend of her brother.

This was a full blown love affair. It was immediately passionate and romantic. He took her everywhere. She met and liked and was liked by his family. They travelled abroad on superb holidays, were always seen together and referred to and invited to places as a couple.

Jennifer gave in completely, decided to enjoy herself and simply let things take their course. But she did this in the firm belief that this time it would be OK.

Why this glorious affair ended she was not sure. One day all was sunny and bright and the next there it was - just an ever so small cloud in an otherwise blue sky. So small was it that she did not see it, but she could and did feel it.

A week or two later, the cloud had materialised. It took the form of Reg excusing himself from one of their many regular nights together. Just the one, but it was the lame excuse.

'Sorry ducks, but if you don't mind I'm a bit knackered.'

Jennifer, as often before, ignored the message.

Before long there were more missed opportunities and more excuses. But an unhappy Jennifer continued to pretend everything was the same - it wasn't.

Eventually things got so bad she decided to confide in her new work colleague. And after work in a local pub she unburdened herself.

'I really don't understand it,' she said.

'Everything seems right, and yet it isn't. He still says he loves me and treats me like a queen, but at the same time shies away from making love.'

Seline, Jennifer's new colleague, looked sympathetic. The affair was well known and often discussed in the office but this turn of events was new, and she had little of value to add.

'Look,' she offered. 'Relationships go through many ups and downs perhaps this is just a temporary thing.'

'Do you have such problems?' Jennifer wanted to know.

After a pause Seline admitted that her own experience with men had been much the same. She had, she said, had several love affairs that had just seemed to peter out.

And she was now without a chap.

'How do you deal with it?' Jennifer asked.

'I just put it down to experience and keep looking.' Seline replied.

An unhappy Jennifer reflected on Seline's situation. The girl was undeniably attractive. Soft blond hair was an appropriate setting for a gentle but vivacious face lit by a pair of startlingly blue eyes. Her figure was full and sensual. Even as they sat at the bar she received many an appraising look. There seemed on the face of it no reason for her to lack male company.

'After all,' Seline added, 'finding out can be fun.' She chuckled and grinned.

On this happier note they finished their drinks and left.

Back at home Jennifer found that Seline's comforting words soon wore off, and deciding to face up to her situation. She realised that her association with Reg was making her unhappy, and concluded that it would continue to do so unless she acted. So of the choices available she made up her mind that it would have to end - and resolved to make this happen first thing the next day.

To her surprise this decision did not cause her the anticipated anguish but she was almost overcome by an overwhelming feeling of relief. It was as if an enormous weight had been lifted from her.

***

As she lay in bed waiting for sleep to take her in its healing embrace she started to ponder what Seline had said.

She turned over in her mind their relative situations and how similar they were. Sleep refused to come and Jennifer spent a restless night, snatches of their conversation going round and round in her mind. Dosing only for a short interval just before dawn, she awoke with a start thinking for a second that she was somewhere else.

As she lay re-orienting herself she gradually sensed a change. Somehow in the throws of the night something very fundamental had happened to her mind. Suddenly, gone were the uncertainties and self doubts, to be replaced by a new, clearer, knowledge of herself.

She lay and allowed the new awareness to become a fact.

Slowly and with some trepidation she climbed out of bed, and walked over to the full length mirror.

She looked, and knew for the first time and with absolute certainty, that the woman looking back at her was -

A lesbian.

The shock was quickly followed by a physical thrill.

It became clear to her that this is what she had been unaware of but which the men in her life had sensed.

She was the same person and yet not the same. And as she got used to the new Jennifer her thoughts turned to Seline and an anticipation filled her from head to loins as she pictured the girl's glorious figure, laughing blue eyes, and obvious femininity.

And she started to dress with great care, impatient for the day to unfold.

JML
3/1/2006

⸙ **FOR WANT OF WEALTH** ⸙

As the senior policeman in charge of the small population of the rather upper strata village of Carrington Super he had an insight into everything that was going on both as gossip and as fact.

Had he made known all he knew several lives would have been very different indeed, but he had taken an oath of confidentiality which he observed punctiliously.

He held the key but did not use it.

Charles Renfrew Copewell was born in the village, had attended school there, and been assigned to the local force almost from the day he joined. He therefore had grown up with his flock and knew them all intimately save, that is, for a dozen or so in-comers.

As a small boy he had seen Giles Willins's father purchase the four acres of rough ground hidden from the village by 'The Woods'. He had taken account of Giles's application to use the space as a scrap metal recovery area with large vehicle access from the main road. And after the usual fight with the council and the regular objectors permission was given.

Charles watched as a teenager as Giles worked hard to turn his scrap metal business into a success. He saw Giles move into Shelly Hall, hire staff, and take on a brand new Bentley with its own driver.

However all this ostentatious parade of wealth did not change Giles one bit; he still enjoyed his regular drink and game of darts at the Unicorn with his pals as before. He was in fact both liked and respected. Not least because of his renowned readiness to buy a round of drinks.

'Set em up again mine host.' Was what the assembled throng loved to hear. And did hear often.

Giles made free with his money.

As far as the unattached (and it has to be said attached) ladies were concerned he was considered a very good catch. But having avoided a permanent relationship Giles reached the ripe old age of thirty-five before he fell for the very appealing wiles of Anthea Turnbull a fairly recent addition to the village.

Anthea, it was generally acknowledged could have had her pick of any of the men but chose the very personable Giles. She did this because she saw that she would inherit considerable wealth and live very well indeed in the meantime. This she made no secret of and fixed their wedding for as soon as she could prise Giles away from his scrap business for a day. They honeymooned at the Hall.

They made a fine couple - but all was not well. Anthea was comely and friendly but she did not enjoy the physical side of life whereas Giles was a normal male and eager to catch up on his deprived years. Some time passed and Giles eventually realised he would die childless and their relationship foundered. But Andrea clung on in the hope of the inheritance.

Meantime our upholder of the law kept his council.

Eventually Giles forced the issue.

'We can't go on like this. We are making each other bloody miserable, and I need an heir, so perhaps you would agree to bugger off.'

It was a demand not a question.

So a divorce was arranged, the financial arrangements were efficiently handled by the local solicitors Young and Son, the contract being negotiated by old Mr. Young.

Now Giles declared that he would not sell the hall it (he declared) being his future son's inheritance so he paid Andrea a handsome income from his scrap business instead.

PC Charles said nothing.

More years passed and Giles began to fret about his age and lack of female company at the Hall where he felt like a pea rattling about in a bucket. He began to spend more time at the Unicorn and was often just a little over the eight.

Then there came to live in the village two ladies both of whom would play a part in Giles's life.

Katherine Keays was a divorcee, and twenty years Giles's junior was still femininely comely with a jolly nature. A regular visitor to the Unicorn she was soon on friendly terms with all especially the men, many of whom entertained lascivious thoughts of the desirable newcomer.

Giles was especially smitten even though she made no bones about being after his estate. And she started to fall for his bluff nature in a big way. The pair were often seen racing round the countryside in the big Bentley or exchanging stories at the bar with much laughter. She was, the village decided, good for him.

And, as nature took its course, he found she was a delight in bed.

But in spite of her requests Giles would not agree to marriage, he felt he wanted proof of a child first. As this did not happen, the issue of marriage began to rankle between them.

And it eventually boiled over.

'When are we going to get married?' Asked Katherine, her pleasant features torn by anguish.

'Why do you want to marry me so bloody badly?' Giles wanted to know.

Riled, Katherine told the truth -

'Because I want your estate when you die.' It was half intended as a joke.

But she got a shock -

'Well you would be wasting your bloody time,' he said, 'I've left the whole caboodle to charity.'

Realising that by now he would be unlikely to have an heir Giles had allowed himself to be persuaded to leave it all to a specific charity.

With real sadness Katherine gathered herself and her belongings and left Giles and the village to look for more profitable game.

Again Giles was kind and his business allowed Katherine to leave with a substantial sum.

Throughout this drama Charles remained silent.

Giles was devastated and wondered if he was doing the right thing. He found out too late how much Katherine had meant to him. For months he went about like a machine without feeling and was seen to smile but rarely, and buried himself in scrap.

Now the cause of all this heartache was the latest addition to the local population. For it was she who had been the agent for the charity to which Giles had left his all.

Addie Wentworth, divorced, young, vital, and very, very attractive, was a quiet lass who kept herself very much to herself. In spite of many an attempt the locals were unable to find out the slightest piece of information about her or her past.

All the eager young men of the village were after her. She was never short of escorts from which she could take her pick. But she chose none of them.

Instead she sought the company of old man Giles, and was often seen in her little red sports car leaving the Hall in the wee small hours.

This brought Giles many a remark in the Unicorn, not all of which were humorous. His association with young Addie caused much envy and some suspicion of ill goings on.

Younger men out with Addie would raise the issue only to be coolly diverted.

'Why do you spend so much time with old man Willins?' One would ask. 'It isn't natural.'

'Now I don't pry into your private life, anyway I can choose my own company. Perhaps you would prefer someone else to be with?' Said with a smile.

And so they would give up asking but not give up asking her out.

Giles's association with Addie eventually became an established and accepted part of village life, which lasted for several years.

The calmness of the place was ripped apart quite suddenly by Giles's unexpected death. The previous evening he had been in the Unicorn having his leg pulled as usual about Addie, and had left at closing time quite merry, and had driven himself home in the Bentley much as usual.

The Hall staff had found him tucked up in bed looking 'unusually tidy' but stone cold and lifeless.

As for all sudden deaths our policeman Charles was called in, and despite the doctor's diagnosis of a massive heart attack was troubled with a niggling doubt.

And to be on the safe side he froze and had sealed all Giles's estate documents including his will. But since the doctor's conclusion of a natural end to Giles's life he did permit the funeral to go ahead.

For the village it was a grand affair, a proper church service followed by burial in the church grounds and a very boozy reception at the Unicorn. Many a tearful and affectionate word was said over a glass of good ale or slug of fine malt. And they had seen the last of good old Giles.

But not everyone.

After the funeral, our PC paid an official visit to the solicitor at the request of young Mr Young who had taken over from old Mr Young.

In preparation for dealing with the Willins's estate he had opened the will which had been prepared by his father and had noticed a strange thing. The whole of the estate was willed to one charity. He had checked that it was a properly registered charity, but it had but a single executive manager - the name being A. Swininggale.

The name, he said, was so unusual it jogged something in his memory. Swininggale was the maiden name of one Addie Wentworth.

Charles's suspicions were aroused.

On making discrete enquiries he discovered that Addie's sports car had been seen leaving the Hall late on the night of Giles's death.

More alarmingly, he found out that Addie had been married before moving to the village and that her husband had met his end under somewhat dubious circumstances leaving her reasonably well off.

Even more worrying was a call from young Mr Young that Addie had been asking when the will would be sorted.

'She sounded quite anxious.' He said.

So after much thought he had Giles's body secretly exhumed one night and submitted for a full forensic check.

However nothing was found and Giles was duly re-interred.

***

Charles realised that he had no choice but to release the estate papers. He decided to attend the reading of Giles's will. He wanted to see the effect of what he already knew and had known over all these years.

The only persons present were Giles's only living relative, a distant and already quite well to do cousin, Addie, for the charity, our PC and young Mr Young.

The sombre atmosphere was charged with tension.

Young Mr Young addressed the silent group.

'The will has been authenticated and is very straight-forward,' he began.

'The whole of the estate goes to The Charity for Young Widows whose sole proprietor and representative is Addie here.' He said with a nod in her direction.

The cousin shrugged, thanked young Mr Young and left.

Addie, now smiling smugly said -

'Well then how much do you reckon it will be?'

The policeman and the solicitor exchanged glances - they knew what was coming.

Young Mr Young took a deep breath.

'All told I estimate that after funeral and other expenses the whole estate will amount to about three thousand pounds.'

A heavy silence filled the room as Addie took this in. Then -

'What?'

Young Mr Young repeated his previous statement this time more slowly.

Another silence gripped them, broken by -

'That can't be right. What about the Hall, the business, the car and all that?' She waved her hand to describe a large spread of wealth. Anger gradually replaced her expression of disbelief as young Mr Young proceeded to explain patiently and precisely.

'All Mr Willins's wealth sprang from his scrap business,' here he paused. 'The Hall and its furnishings were leased from Lord Henry's Estate. The Bentley was hired on a monthly basis.' He waited, but Addie said nothing.

'Most of the income from the business went on these outgoings plus his regular contribution to his divorced wife.'

This time a long silence.

'I'm sorry.' Said the young Mr Young merely to break the tension.

Addie for once looked old and shattered as she saw her schemes dribble away to almost nothing.

With an obvious effort she gathered herself together and with all the dignity she could muster stood and thanked the young Mr Young, gave him a card with her forwarding address, said goodbye, shook his hand and left.

Once outside the room the two men heard her curse.

'The rotten old miser, I hope his soul rots in hell.'

They listened as the drumming of her sports car faded into the distance, to be replaced by the village's gentle peace.

The young Mr young looked at Charles.

'You could have told her.' He said mildly. 'You could have told all of them.' He added. 'You knew all the time.'

'I know said Charles.'

JML
10/1/2006

❧ **THE LECTURE PRIZE** ☙

The College founder, a keen politician and believer in free speech had sought to encourage and improve the level of debate by setting aside a substantial sum of money from which a prize was to be awarded each year to the best lecture given by a student. The staff would be the only and ultimate judges and an antique glass vase, known as 'the spittoon' accompanied the cash.

In spite of the members of the students union denigrating the award, and its contributors, competition was fierce.

In fact so strong was the desire to win that on one notorious occasion a foul and despicable plot was hatched to ruin the chances of one worthy challenger.

In fact so bad was the evil deed judged that the perpetrators humped their belongings and shuffled ignominiously off home never to show their faces inside the hallowed walls again.

It came about thus-wise.

The victim was one Gervaise Pellen Rekaeps known universally as Gerry.

Now students of the college were not given much to seriousness but as seriousness goes Gerry was it in person.

He was the last to see a joke and often had to request an explanation.

'Hay Gerry, my brother is still living at home at 35 and my old man was getting fed up, so he said to him, 'Isn't it time you took a wife?' 'Great idea,' said my brother, 'whose wife do you suggest?'

Poor old Gerry looks mystified and says, 'It's wrong to pinch another's wife - why should your father recommend such a course of action?'

You see the problem.

And because of this and his willing nature Gerry was the butt of more than his fair share of leg pulls and practical jokes.

And bless his brave heart and naivety Gerry entered himself for the 'Spittoon' lecture competition.

Now the lady of the piece was one Cherryl (Cherry) Rekool admired and chased by close on 100% of the Colleges male fraternity. Not good looking in a conventional way, she nevertheless simply was the very essence of womanhood. She represented mother, mistress and slick professional all rolled into a single gorgeous package. And she had no time for fools or braggarts.

Top of the list of the latter, Bartholemu Guht known to all as Batts. Batts had of course set his sights on harvesting Cherry, spending time, energy and money on doing so. But to little avail, since our Cherry the darling girl she was not only liked the nervous and self affacing Gerry but was steadily falling for him.

Batts and his cronies (such people always seem to collect a group of hangers on) took every possible opportunity to raise their standing in College especially at the expense of poor old Gerry.

And Batts seemed to be winning. He was good at all sports, a tolerable boxer, a sociable drinker and frequent teller of bawdy jokes; none of which Gerry aspired to. In fact it was locally considered that in the chase for Cherry, Batts had her in the bag, whereas Gerry was nowhere to be seen.

Batts of course had to win. However his academic abilities did not allow him the slightest chance of gaining the spittoon, he could barely hold an intelligent conversation let alone give a lecture; so he resolved to find another way - and this he did.

Gerry's talk was duly scheduled and posters advertising its unappetising title appeared on every spare space. The prospective audience were invited to 'Ancient Viking Writing - Its Effect on Current Language'. On this announcement the hot money went on Gerry as it was thought that this was just the sort of thing that would score highly in the eyes of the staff.

Gerry worked hard and long in his preparation, but so did Batts and his cohorts.

At the rear of the lecture theatre a video camera was mounted out of sight but high enough to capture the stage and most of the auditorium. This was plugged into the college system and a linked monitor was placed facing the audience in an alternative lecture room. Would-be attenders of the lecture were told in secret and under the pain of terrible penalties if any word of this was breathed to poor old Gerry.

And so the die was cast.

An eager and giggling audience slowly gathered in the alternative theatre and gazed fascinated at the monitor showing an empty stage with a lectern facing row upon row of empty seats.

Only one seat was occupied, for fear of a leak Cherry had not been told.

To be fair to Batts his organisation had worked perfectly - but just not quite, there was one very small oversight; and they thought they knew our Gerry.

The remote audience waited and as the time for Gerry's appearance grew near the hum of conversation dwindled and eventually ceased. Anticipation gripped the room. Someone giggled and was promptly given a loud 'Sh'.

Then this lonely figure clutching his notes walked out on to the stage, paused and turned to face the empty room.

Students in the other room held their breath - what the hell would he do?

Well there he stood all alone, puzzled and visibly upset.

He stood for a seemingly very long time. The other room was silent in anticipation, had he guessed he was being watched?

Suddenly the tension was broken as Gerry hurled his notes into the air where they floated like leaves down around him.

A cheer went up in the other room.

But instead of walking off Gerry continued to stand there.

Silence descended again in the other room.

Time ticked on.

Then gripping the lectern with both hands Gerry, quietly at first, began to speak.

This was unexpected and a murmur was quickly hushed.

'This is just what is wrong with the world today. Competition will destroy us.' He paused thinking, then -

'Think about it. For every winner there has to be a looser. And what do you think it does for the looser? Does it give him an impetus to do better? Not bloody likely. It is more inclined to eat into his very soul, denigrating his assumed position in the scheme of things.

Not only does this apply to individuals but to colleges, countries and governments.'

At this a few people decided that what Gerry had to say might be worth listening to, even if not he was definitely out to say his piece, so they left the alternative theatre and quietly transferred themselves to Gerry's.

Gerry was now in full tilt and speaking with real feeling.

'It seems to me that it is failure to win that forces all kinds of organisations - industry, states, unions of all sorts, even religions, to fight back with every kind of warfare.'

This was good stuff, and more people joined Gerry and his theatre was becoming quite full.

'How many individuals do we know who have resigned, retired, and even taken their own or other people's lives due to having failed in some competitive struggle?

Even families are not immune, sibling rivalry has been responsible for some of histories most terrible misdeeds.'

Gerry's room was now full with standing room only for late arrivals. Left alone in the alternative were Batts and one or two hangers on.

Gerry was in full flood.

'And what of the winners? Does it improve them? Not likely. They stand higher in their own estimation smug in the knowledge of the opposition's defeat and now with the knowledge of power gained and ready to be used for good or evil. And sadly all too often for evil.'

Gerry presented his case with an eloquence born of certainty and with fire born of conviction. He made a powerful case with many a telling quotation and illustrative example.

The audience took to him. He was clapped often and frequently cheered.

Gerry held his audience entranced for an hour when sheer exhaustion eventually brought him to a close, and to his astonishment he was mobbed by admiring students as he left the theatre.

In the other room Batts was dumfounded, not being all that bright he really did not understand what had gone wrong. But for him worse was to come. As for Gerry things seemed to get even better but he should have listened to his own lecture.

***

Unbeknownst to either Bratt or Gerry there was a another monitor attached to the video circuit which was for the exclusive use by the staff and was sighted in a much more sumptuous room where they had sat and watched the whole proceedings in relative comfort.

The upshot of this was that after a brief discussion the staff members unanimously agreed to award the spittoon Lecture Prize to Gerry.

They also agreed that at the end of term it was to be suggested to Batts and one or two others that they might be happier elsewhere.

Batts dropped all attempts to attract the one and only Cherry.

And did Gerry win the fair maid?

No he did not.

As stated before he should have noted his own speech.

Cherry had loved the awkward, misunderstood, shy and unworldly lad. He brought out the mother in her, she wanted to protect him from the harsh world, to coddle and nurture him. She loved his quiet even simple nature.

But this winner of the spittoon was a different person altogether. Confident, brave, dogmatic, the new Gerry thought he could simply beckon Cherry and she would come - but she declined, and found someone else more deserving of her care. She felt that Gerry simply didn't have a need for her any more.

Poor Gerry never worked out what he was doing wrong, but he bravely put his disappointment behind him and his new self served him quite well through his future life.

Nothing further is know about Batts.

JML
16/1/2006

⊰ **THE TRAP** ⊱

Sandy Beldini and Michael Strang were in fear for their lives - and with good reason.

They had met and had instantly fallen in love which was an extremely dangerous thing to do, but they could not help it, it just happened as fate sometimes dictates.

The trouble was that for the last three years Sandy was married to Joe Beldini.

A glorious holiday in Italy by the side of Lake Como had thrust Sandy into the bosom of the Beldini clan. She dined at their lakeside restaurant and at her very first visit was commandeered by Joe who was also there from England, visiting his family, and was thus free to pursue the luckless young lady.

What appealed to Joe was the Englishness of Sandy; blond and hazel eyed with a pale almost transparent skin so different from the local girls he usually took out. Her shy and self conscious nature also contrasted favourably with the usually garrulous Italian maidens.

Now Joe, the family youngest, was thoroughly spoilt and was very used to getting his own way. As Sandy discovered too late. He would also stop at nothing to get that which he had set his mind on; when winning he was happy, oozed charm, and was excellent company.

And Joe made sure that Sandy fell for him. And she did.

Joe was in a hurry and the first time Sandy's parents met Joe and his large family was at their wedding in Italy. It was too late for Sandy's father to warn her of what he suspected Joe was capable of, he could only pray for his love-struck daughter.

Joe and Sandy returned to England and set up home.

Sadly her father was not wrong. Joe proved to be fanatically jealous and demanding of his marital rights. Each love making was nothing short of rape, after which Sandy would cry herself to sleep whilst not daring to let Joe see she was unhappy. He was suspicious of Sandy's every move. He would want to know in detail every little thing she had done whilst out of his sight. Frequent unwarranted suspicions brought her threats of terrible physical punishments which he reinforced by actual beatings.

When out together any suggestion of a mere glance in the direction of another male would send Joe into a paroxysm of rage with a few blows later to reinforce his point and vent his frustration.

Also, she had no idea where Joe's obvious wealth came from and any enquiries were angrily discouraged.

Sensitively brought up by loving parents to look forward to a happy marriage - Sandy was very, very unhappy.

Then she met Michael.

Their meeting was innocent enough.

Sandy was shopping in town and had called for a coffee at a small roadside cafe, it was busy and the tables were full.

She had just sat down when Michael wandered over and asked if she would mind awfully if he took one of the spare seats at her table.

Sandy took a nervous look round to see if Joe was anywhere in sight, and hesitated. Then fatefully -

'Not at all,' she said, 'please do.'

Michael took the seat opposite Sandy, looked into her eyes and was immediately and completely captivated. In fact he was stunned, he thought that he had never seen anyone so perfectly matching his ideal. He simply sat and filled his gaze with her magic.

Suddenly it dawned on him that he was behaving extremely rudely which was not his normal behaviour and so he apologised.

'I'm very sorry,' he said, 'I really don't mean to stare, you must think me awfully rude.'

Now Sandy had subconsciously responded to Michael with a whirlwind reaction of her own, which took her by surprise.

Her response was as natural as it was heart felt.

'No it's quite all right.' Then after a pause, 'I really don't mind in the least.'

Michael's heart leapt, and after placing his order for coffee with the waitress, he jumped right in.

'My name is Michael, and forgive me but,' then in a rush, 'would you let me take you for lunch?'

Sandy should have been surprised but wasn't. What she was was enormously attracted to this clean, honest looking young man with the most endearing smile and mischievous grin.

But Joe's influence was everywhere. She overcame her fear with difficulty and after a nervous look around breathlessly agreed to let Michael buy her lunch.

They ate at a nearby pub, and soon found that they liked each other's company very much indeed, but their pleasure was almost ruined by Sandy's constantly checking to see if Joe or any of his cronies had seen them.

Mutual love had taken over and was about to spiral them into a vortex of passion and fear.

Sandy was honest from the start and told Michael of Joe and her unhappy marriage to him. She made him understand that not only her life was at risk but his also should Joe ever even suspect that the knew each other let alone were in love.

Michael was free of any attachments and was all too eager to whisk her away and make her his. A very dangerous ambition indeed.

After some discussion they agreed to meet in places well away from her and Joe's home and well out in open park land where they could see anyone spying on them. Sandy insisted that Michael ensured that he was not followed, and she made certain that neither was she.

At first Michael thought that Sandy was exaggerating the risk, but he did acknowledge that her fear was real enough. So they met in great secrecy and eventually became lovers.

Back at home Joe was worse. Whether it was an extra glint in Sandy's eye or a swift smile caught when she thought Joe wasn't looking, but he became very suspicious and frequently threatened her with death.

'Don't youse think I don' know what you'r up to you tart. De boys is on to you. Jus' let em catch you even sayin' 'hallo' to some slimy bastard and I'll send you both to hell.'

And with face twisted in anger, 'I know everythin'. De boys'll see to you if I don'.'

Sandy would go ice-cold with fear. She knew he meant every word, and regarded the future with dread.

She and Michael discussed all the options, but at each suggestion they could not avoid Joe and his threats.

Matters were getting desperate and Joe was getting more suspicious, when out of the blue the situation seemed to get much much worse.

Joe arrived home clearly in a unusual mood, almost jolly, very relaxed and almost civil. After dinner he brought her a drink and invited Sandy to join him, which he had never done before.

Then the bombshell.

'De family wan' me to do some business abroad,' he announced. 'So I'll be away about three weeks.'

He waited for her comment but got none.

'De plane leaves tomorrow evenin.'

Still no reaction from Sandy which made him suspicious and angry again.

'An don you tink yuose can do your like. I've asked de boys to a check on you all de bloody time. You won' change your pants widou' me findin' out. An then......'

He left the rest unsaid.

Sandy tried hard not to show the fear and hope fighting inside her in equal measure, but managed -

'I hope you have a good trip, where is it to?'

She should have known better, Joe's response was an angry -

'I tol' you, jus' abroad.'

All the next day Joe made preparations to leave. He gathered documents, made seemingly endless phone calls in Italian, double checked his cash and passport, and in the early evening climbed into the large black limousine that duly called for him; and was gone. His only parting words were typical Joe.

'Don forget. De boys is watchin'.'

A day later Sandy and Michael met under a lone oak in a very empty park. It was sunny and warm but Sandy was chill with apprehension.

'It's a trap,' she said. 'It's a trap, I just know it is. He wouldn't tell me where he was going and made such a fuss about finding his passport. I think he's still here and just waiting to catch us.'

She was close to tears.

For Michael this was new territory. No previous experience would guide him and he was at a loss as to know what course of action to take. With a deep feeling of inadequacy he tried to comfort Sandy. He was however certain of one thing - he was not going to loose her now he had found her.

They discussed every option but in the end decided to keep meeting as before and leave any more conclusive action until after Joe's return.

So the days of Joe's absence slipped by.

Every couple of days Sandy received a much travelled postcard with a picture of some non-descript hotel, Italian stamp, and with the written words 'Don't forget'.

Sandy and Michael met and were doubly cautious.

Just two weeks into Joe's absence Sandy got the first of three shattering visits.

It was early morning. A knock at the door. She opened it and without even a glance at Sandy three hard looking men burst in and immediately went through the house checking no doubt that she was on her own.

One guarded the door whilst the other two, not unkindly sat her down and started to ask her questions.

From their accents they were clearly Italian. They were very insistent and wanted to know her every movement since Joe left. Who had visited the house. Had she made any phone calls abroad. Had she received any calls from abroad. Then abruptly they left.

Sandy was shaken, and discussing it with Michael was convinced this was set up by Joe to frighten her.

Michael was not so sure, and if anything was more frightened than Sandy. Perhaps she was right and it was a trap set up to catch them out, but perhaps it was altogether something more sinister.

Then a second shock arrived unannounced and shattering.

Sandy on her own out shopping took a short cut down a narrow passage between buildings. Without warning a hand grabbed her and spun her round to face two men whose faces were hidden by scarves. A knife was flashed inches from her face and one of then said - 'Don' scream lady or I'll change your lovely face for you, see.'

Sandy was too frightened to scream. Their accents were Italian and she knew who had sent them, and expected the worst.

'Now we know what youse bin up to, so if you value your life you'd best give us what we want.'

This was it she thought.

'Where's Joe?'

The question took her aback.

'You know where he is,' she managed, 'he sent you.'

The men exchanged glances and she felt the point of the blade at her throat.

'Don be bloody clever. Where the hell is he? Tell us or else, we jus' wan' a little chat wid 'im - see.'

Sandy was too frightened to think and started to cry.

'Believe me,' she said. 'He never told me anything.'

The two men held a brief discussion in Italian, then one of them said.

'Yea, that would be Joe, but youse tellin' us wrong we'll sort you. Understand?'

With that they were gone leaving Sandy holding on to the wall and shaking.

Later in the comfort of Michael's arms she recovered enough to tell him what had happened.

'I told you,' she said. 'It's part of Joe's trap to catch us, these men mean business.'

Michael was not so sure, to him it did not stack up, but he had no better explanation.

They went about life with a wariness born of real fear, waiting for the axe to fall at any moment. Sandy was afraid to answer the door and even the telephone She went out as little as possible and kept to busy streets. Michael, much to his distress kept away.

***

At the end of the third week of Joe's absence Sandy opened the door to three smartly dressed official looking men. They were studiously polite, introduced themselves as police, waived warrant cards at her, waited patiently whilst she phoned to check they were who they said they were, then produced a search warrant.

One of the men asked her to sit down, then -

'I'm Bill Jenkin, and I'm sorry about this but we have to act on information received.'

He paused. Then that question again.

'Can you tell me if you know where Joe has been?'

She convinced him that she did not know where Joe had been or where he was now. Meanwhile the other two returned from their search, shook their heads at Sandy's interrogator, excused themselves and left.

After a long silence whilst the policeman seemed to be collecting himself, he said -

'I know where Joe is, and I'm afraid I have some very bad news for you. You may need a drink.'

Sandy was taken aback, but managed to ask him to continue.

'We believe your husband has been killed...... his body is being flown back here......... and we would like you to identify him.'

This was not right, Joe, tough self willed Joe, Joe always the boss just couldn't be dead.

Sandy just sat there. The policeman waited politely.

'Where? What happened?'

The policeman hesitatingly told the story as they understood it, and Sandy listened without interruption.

'I'm afraid he was found by the Italian police at the house of a young prostitute. He had been shot three times in the chest from close range. It was an execution.

It seems that the Beldini family had for some time suspected Joe of cheating them at their game of money laundering and was syphoning a nice pile for himself, which incidentaly we are still looking for.'

His next words astonished Sandy.

'So the Beldini's set a trap for him. A trap that he fell right into. They knew of his taste for very young girls and managed to get one to get him to talk, and he spilled the beans and that sealed his fate. The Italian police have the Beldini's and they will stand trial for murder.'

Sandy just sat trying to take it all in.

The policeman rose, handed Sandy his card and told her that he would be in touch, and turned to leave. Then -

'Why don't you get your friend, er .... Michael, isn't it to come over?......... I don't think you will be having any more trouble from the Beldini's............Well goodbye for the present. I'll let myself out.'

JML
22/1/2006

✦ **THE WAY MONEY GOES ROUND** ✦

*J*im the site manager had just arrived at the building site and unlocked his small office when the phone rang and the secretary announced that his boss was on his way over to see him. He was apprehensive about the visit but confident as the job was going well.

The boss and part owner of the company strode in without knocking, sat down in the one spare chair and demanded a mug of tea. That in hand, as a no frills man he jumped straight in.

'Things look good and we have decided to pay you a small bonus. Well done and thanks for the good work.'

With this he gulped his tea, dropped an envelope onto the cluttered desk, said cheerio and left.

As the envelope had his name and address on it Jim gingerly picked it up and using his sandwich knife sliced it open. Inside he discovered twenty neat tenners. £200, very nice he thought, Jean will be delighted and might just wear that new frilly nighty she was saving for a special occasion.

He had an early appointment with a supplier, so he hurriedly slipped the envelope into the pocket of his old top-coat, and taking his car set off for town. Unfortunately as he clambered out of the car the envelope slipped out of the coat pocket where it lay unnoticed by Jim on the pavement.

Just after Jim had returned to his car and driven off the envelope was spotted by Danny who, after a quick look round, picked it up. He was delighted at his little windfall and made instant and rapid steps to the bookies.

Now Danny was well known at the bookies and his bets were refused unless he could show that he had the means to cover them.

He took out the notes, waved them at the man behind the counter, replaced them in the envelope, pocketed it in his mac pocket, and made his bet. But all this had been carefully observed by Alexy.

To Danny's and everyone else's surprise his horse came in at three to one, so even after tax he had made a very nice profit. He collected his money and stuffed it firmly in his inside pocket where he knew it would be safe.

As Danny left the bookies closely followed by Alexy he decided he would buy that car he had his eye on and surprise the wife; and who knows it might put her in the mood for some fun later.

Now Alexy was a dip and a gambler, and Alexy badly needed funds. So as he apologised to Danny for bumping into him he lifted the envelope still with its £200 from Danny's Mac pocket.

Danny went on to buy the car, missed the envelope but had enough from his winnings so he shrugged the loss off and with a chuckle drove home in his new possession.

Alexy hurried to join a very dubious card game. He sat down with the other three grey looking individuals, and at a prompt showed them the envelope and its contents.

He was unusually lucky and more than doubled his stake and for once stopped before he was tempted to stay on for more and lose it.

The money he split, placing the original £200 back in the envelope and into his anorak pocket, the rest he hid in his boots.

As he left he thought that he might just have enough to pull that nice blond chick at the pub, and still have the original envelope and its contents.

As Alexy left the game and slid down the back alley he was suddenly accosted by two youths. They forced him up against the wall at knife point and quickly found the envelope. However, just then two policemen ran towards them and the lads fled. They made for the main street where the one with the ill gotten gains decided to get rid of the incriminating evidence and threw the envelope and contents aside. The policemen lost the lads, and the envelope dropped on the pavement were it was seen and picked up by Edward.

Edward was a minor clerk in an estate agency. He also dabbled in a very small way on the stock market. As it happened he had his eye on a company that he felt was ripe for a take over. But as all his available funds were tied up in shares which he was reluctant to sell he thought that he would have to let the opportunity pass. Here however was a small miracle. It was just before lunch when Edward placed his order to buy with his broker, placed the envelope on top of the correspondence on his desk to be dealt with later, and left the office for his mid-day break.

Back at his desk, he was enjoying a mid afternoon cup of tea when his broker rang. The take over had been announced, the shares had trebled what should he do?

Edward did not hesitate.

'Sell them now please.'

Later the broker phoned again.

'Cleared at over three times,' he said, 'even after our commission it will mean a tidy profit.'

Now Edward would not need the money in the envelope, and reached for it - but it was not there.

Whilst he was out, the office apprentice had been round collecting correspondence for posting and seeing the envelope addressed and stamped had picked it up and added it to the post bag and was even now on his way to the post office.

As far as Edward was concerned the money was no longer needed and he looked forward with pleasurable anticipation to his wife's expected thanks for his being able to tell her they could now afford the deposit an that house she had set her mind on.

Meanwhile the office apprentice decided to post the letters at a nearby post box instead of the longer walk to the main post office. As he struggled with the bundle, one dropped unseen to the floor and was kicked by a passer-by to come to rest half hidden under the door of a nearby empty shop. It still had its contents intact.

A youth passing by later, spotted the envelope and out of curiosity picked it up.

***

During all this, our good friend Jim, the site manager, had not missed his envelope when home time came. On his return he decided to surprise his wife with his good news later. Thus he hung up his coat unaware that its pockets were empty.

It was in the middle of their evening meal when the front door bell rang.

Jim opened the door and saw standing there supporting his bike with one hand and holding Jim's envelope in the other was a youth of about thirteen.

To say Jim was astonished would be an understatement he could not imagine what the lad was doing with his envelope.

The boy found his tongue.

'I found this in the high street. Its got money in it.

It has this address on it.'

Jim took the envelope in a daze and checked the contents. All the money was there. His relief was profound.

'How far have you come?' He managed.

'About two miles.' The lad said.

Jim removed a tenner from the envelope and handed it to the grateful youth.

'Well many many thanks,' he said. 'Please take this you've earned it.'

'Gee. Thanks mister.' And he was gone.

Later Jim reaped the gentle rewards from his wife.

And the lad thought erotic thoughts on how he would impress Maisy come the weekend.

JML
25/1/2006

ISBN 141208652-3